Being Bee

Catherine Bateson

Holiday House / New York

For Belinda Jane Chisholm

© Catherine Bateson 2006

First published 2006 by University of Queensland Press, Box 6042,
St. Lucia, Queensland 4067 Australia

First published in the United States of America by Holiday House, Inc.
in 2007

All Rights Reserved

Printed in the United States of America

www.holidayhouse.com

1   3   5   7   9   10   8   6   4   2

Library of Congress Cataloging-in-Publication Data

Bateson, Catherine, 1960-

Being Bee / by Catherine Bateson.

p. cm.

Summary: Bee faces friction at home and at school when her
widowed father begins seriously dating Jazzi, who seems to take
over the house and their lives, but as shared secrets and common
interests finally begin to draw them together, Jazzi accidentally
makes a terrible mistake.

ISBN-13: 978-0-8234-2104-6 (hardcover)

ISBN-10: 0-8234-2104-X (hardcover)

[1. Family life–Australia–Fiction. 2. Widowers–Fiction.
3. Friendship–Fiction. 4. Schools–Fiction. 5. Guinea pigs–Fiction.
6. Mentally ill–Fiction. 7. Australia–Fiction.]   I. Title.

PZ7.B3222Bei 2007

[Fic]–dc22

2006101561

Guinea pigs rule the world

I didn't mean to shove Lulu, my guinea pig, at Jazzi, my dad's girlfriend, which is what she told Dad. I meant to place Lulu carefully in her hands but her hands weren't exactly where I expected, so Lulu slipped onto the floor of the cubby where she and Fifi are kept. I thought Lulu might have broken her back so I wailed quite loudly. Jazzi said she thought the noise was a fire siren and she nearly stepped on Lulu who was skittering around the cubbyhouse looking for cover.

"It was all quite sudden," Jazzi told my dad with a pinched look on her face. Scrabbling around after Lulu had put a big hole in the knee of her shiny black tights

1

and then she'd kind of plonked down on some straw soaked in guinea pig pee, which hadn't improved her temper. I picked most of the straw off the back of her skirt.

"Oh, Bee!" Dad said, shaking his head.

"I do think the cage needs cleaning out," Jazzi said, "and it does seem to be a job that Beatrice would be able to do. When I was her age I was allowed to have a puppy but only as long as I could look after it all by myself. And that meant cleaning up her messes while I house-trained her. I walked her every day, washed and brushed her, bought her food out of my pocket money and fed her. Cleaning out a guinea pig cage is nothing."

"What was your dog's name?"

"Pepi," Jazzi said, "she was such a sweet little thing. I loved her."

"What happened to her?" I asked.

"Oh," Jazzi looked down at her mug of tea, "you know, she died. It was an accident."

"What happened?"

"She was hit by a car."

"That's really sad."

"Oh, well, it was years ago now, Beatrice."

"Still," I said, "it takes time to get over these things."

"Well, it was years and years ago. Gosh, darling, how old do you think I am? I was your age when I got Pepi."

I looked at her. You can't tell how old grown-ups are. They're either old or very old or sometimes very very old. Jazzi had dark hair, kind of wavy, and there was this cool red streak in it. But someone had chopped the fringe so it looked too short and not very straight. She had dark eyes with shadows underneath them. She had two little creases on either side of her mouth which was all purpley with lipstick so it looked as though she'd been eating plums. Her earrings were big silvery hoops, the kind someone not *very* old would wear.

"Old," I said. "You know, not very very old like Nanna, and probably younger than Dad, but still pretty old."

"Thank you, Beatrice!"

Dad laughed and passed her the plate of biscuits. They were special cream-centered ones but Jazzi shook her head and passed it back to him, missing out on me entirely.

"You have to get used to Bee," Dad said, passing me the biscuits. "She's a bit . . . direct."

"That's what is lovely about children, isn't it? Their honesty." Jazzi smiled at me but the smile only pulled up her mouth.

"That's one way of looking at it," Dad said. "Some of us wish they'd learn some tact. Bee, I think Jazzi is quite right. It is about time you took care of your guinea pigs yourself. Why don't you go down and make a start at cleaning up their cage?"

"Do I have to?"

"Goodness, Bee. Yes, you do. I tell you what, if you clean out their cage really well, I'll give you a couple of dollars, okay?"

"Well, who's a lucky girl?" Jazzi looked at me. "There's an offer you can't refuse!"

It was on the tip of my tongue to do just that. But I looked at Jazzi and Dad and saw they were holding hands, right near the biscuits, which probably meant they'd kiss each other soon and who wanted to be around for that?

"Five dollars?" I said.

"Two," Dad said, giving me one of those looks that said *Don't push it, kiddo.*

"Four." I narrowed my eyes the way baddies did in movies, right before they pulled out their guns.

"Two dollars and fifty cents and that's my final offer. Otherwise you'll do it simply because they are your guinea pigs and I'm sick of cleaning up their mess."

I knew when I was beaten.

"You're a lovely dad," Jazzi was saying as I went out the double doors to the backyard. "And it must be so hard, Nick, by yourself. I don't know how you do it."

It was warm in the cubbyhouse. Fifi and Lulu squeaked when they heard me coming. They always did that. I took Fifi out. It was her turn.

When my mum was still alive, we had the cubby-house set up as a real cubby, with a little table, two chairs, and a shelf that held a tea set. I used to have tea parties there with my friends. I know, because there are photos that show us sitting at the table drinking tea from the tiny cups.

I stopped using the cubby after Mum died. My friends didn't come around as much. So when Dad gave in and bought me Lulu and Fifi, we decided that the cubbyhouse was the best place for their hutch, because of foxes and the cold. I knew they'd feel safer in the cubbyhouse, the way I feel safe in my bed in my own room. They'd look up at night, and there, beyond their little wire roof, would be the big roof and even a little window so they could see the stars. Dad and I took the table and chairs down to the thrift shop. We put the guinea pig food on the shelf and when I got a book on keeping guinea pigs, I kept that there too.

It took ages to clean up the guinea pig mess. I put all the dirty straw and shredded paper in the compost bin and even swept underneath the hutch itself. When I'd finished, the whole afternoon had practically gone.

But when I went back inside, Jazzi was still there, fussing around in the kitchen.

"Aha, the guinea pig trainer returns!" Dad said. "Guess what, love. Jazzi's making us scones for afternoon tea. What do you think of that?"

"Good." Honestly, Dad made it sound as though Jazzi was doing something absolutely marvelous. Nanna made scones for us lots of times and Dad just grunted or muttered about his cholesterol.

But Jazzi's scones weren't the jam-and-cream cholesterol kind. They were weird.

"Savory scones," she said, dumping a plate in the center of the table, "and they haven't quite risen the way I imagined. I'm not familiar with your oven, Nick."

"Delicious," Dad said, immediately stuffing one into his mouth. "Such a treat, Jazzi!"

They were kind of disgusting, actually. There was something hot in them that burned my mouth and you just had butter on them, no jam or anything. Weird. I said that out loud. I didn't mean to be rude. I was just telling the truth.

"You need to develop your palate," Jazzi said.

"Too many Big Macs," Dad said, glaring at me, "that's the trouble. Sugar in everything these days."

"You eat Big Macs!" I said.

Dad and I sometimes had McDonald's breakfasts, when he'd slept in.

"The convenience factor." Dad made a strange face at me before turning to Jazzi and changing it into a droopy kind of smile. "We're so rushed sometimes."

"Of course, I understand," Jazzi said and covered his hand with hers. "You just don't have time for all that.

I love cooking. Always have. Even living by myself, I take the trouble. Food is a celebration for the senses."

I rolled my eyes. Jazzi's scones weren't a celebration for anything but the compost bin as far as I was concerned, but Dad gamely ate three of them. Three!

"Now, darling," Dad said when Jazzi excused herself to use the bathroom, "Jazzi might stay for dinner. That would be okay with you, wouldn't it?"

"Who's cooking?"

"She's offered to. I'm going to drive up to the supermarket and she's going to do us all a lovely stir-fry. You will try to be polite about that, won't you?"

"I wasn't being rude, Dad, I was just being honest. I like ordinary scones the way Nanna makes them."

"Okay, okay, that's enough. Don't worry about being honest, Bee. Just be polite."

"But you always say . . ."

"Shh, she's coming back."

Jazzi came into the kitchen, smiling brightly. "Everything okay, Nick?"

After dinner, Dad asked Jazzi if she wanted to go for an evening stroll. Dad and I often go into Sherbrook Forest. Sometimes you see lyrebirds and wallabies there. It's my favorite place in the whole world.

"Oh, let's do that! I'll get my shoes on."

"Bee," Dad said, "I wasn't really asking you. I'm sorry, sweetheart, but I was asking Jazzi."

"What? We always go together."

I couldn't believe he'd just leave me behind like that. It's what my best friends Sally and Lucy do when they're sick of being a threesome.

"Oh," Jazzi said, "she must come, Nick. We can't just leave her at home by herself."

So in the end I went too, but Dad and Jazzi talked too much and we didn't see even one lyrebird and only heard a wallaby as it thumped away from their voices.

"This is one of the reasons I moved here," Jazzi said. "On my afternoons off I often come up here to relax."

"It is beautiful," Dad said and he moved closer to her as though he wanted to kiss her.

"Look," I said, "there's a big spider on that fern."

They kissed later anyway and I had to pretend to be very interested in some little birds I couldn't even see properly.

They were still kissing when I came out of my room really late that night to get a drink of water. The stir-fry had been hot and made me thirsty.

"Sorry," I said, ducking my head and scooting around them.

"That's okay, Beatrice, it's your house. Don't apologize." Jazzi's voice sounded gentler and when I looked up at her quickly she even looked different, as though kissing Dad had softened her face.

She didn't stay like that. In the morning, when I went into Dad's room to get him to open the juice, she shrieked as though I were armed and dangerous.

"Nick, doesn't she knock?" she said, pulling the sheets up to her chin.

"Bee!" Dad sounded angry. "You can't just barge in. You have to learn some manners."

"And can you turn the TV down a little bit," Jazzi added. "It's up pretty loud for a Sunday morning."

"Actually, turn it off, Bee. You watch far too much of it."

I didn't even know Jazzi was still there. It wasn't fair. They could have warned me, even if they'd left a note on the fridge: *Jazzi is sleeping over.*

I went outside and her car was there, all dusty and rusty and falling apart. It was one of those cars people write *Please clean me* on the back window. I hunched down beside it. It looked as if this car would be at our place a lot. I didn't like her. I didn't like the way she called me Beatrice.

"It's such a lovely old-fashioned name," she said, smiling down at me the day we first met. "I think I will have to call you Beatrice. Someone should."

I didn't know then that she would end up kissing my dad in the kitchen, or staying the night in our house. If I had known, I'd have insisted she call me Bee, like everyone else.

I knew this wouldn't have happened if my mum had still been alive, and I scratched around in the dirt for a while, feeling nearly sad enough to cry, but not quite. I was too angry.

They'd made me miss my all-time favorite TV show, and they didn't care. They weren't even watching TV. They were just in bed, probably talking soppy stuff together. I scratched some of the dust off the bumper bar of Jazzi's car. Then I scratched a really small *Bee Rox* right down on the bumper bar where no one would see it. It looked cool. I did a bigger one and then drew an arrow to a smiley with pigtails. Then I drew a heart with *J Loves N* in it and an arrow through it. Finally I wrote *Guinea Pigs Rule the World!* right across the back window. I just got carried away.

Dad said later that it wasn't that he thought I'd committed a crime, it was just that he wanted to help Jazzi by washing her car for her and he didn't see why I shouldn't help, as I'd been the one to draw attention to the dust in the first place. But it was her car, so why did I have to help?

"Because you are going to be pleasant and helpful, Bee, and not chase Jazzi away. I like Jazzi. I want her to be a permanent fixture in our lives and I don't want any bratty, selfish behavior from you spoiling things. You're going to think of someone else first for once in your life. Do you understand me?"

I understood the words, all right. What I didn't understand was what I'd done. I wished that I'd scratched *Guinea Pigs Rule the World* right across her car doors with something really sharp instead of just drawn it in the dust with an old blunt stick.

Kissing and knitting

"It's not that I don't like her," I told Lucy and Sally at recess. "She's okay. It's just that Dad's different when she's around, and he wants to do things with her and not with me. They kiss all the time, too."

"Eeuuww." Lucy screwed up her face.

"Well, they have to," Sally said, rolling her eyes at us, "they're going out. That's what people do."

"But not when other people are watching," Lucy said.

"Well, my brother and his girlfriend do it all the time," Sally said.

"In front of you?"

"Not always, only sometimes."

"I think it's disgusting," I said. "Dad and Jazzi aren't even young."

"That's a point," Sally said. "It is more horrible when old people do it."

"I think it's just completely yucky," Lucy said. "And I'm not going to let anyone kiss me."

"But what happens when you've got a boyfriend?" All the teachers told Sally she was the practical one. She always asked the sensible questions.

"I'm not having a boyfriend," Lucy said. "I don't like boys. They smell."

"I might kiss someone," I said, trying to imagine what it would be like. "But I won't do it in front of anyone else."

"I bet you do," Sally said. "I bet you a million dollars."

"You don't have a million dollars."

"Anyway, my mum says you need to grow up a bit. She says you're becoming a little bit . . . a little bit . . . I can't remember. It was a word beginning with '*e*' but basically it means weird."

"I'm not weird. I'm no weirder than you are!"

"*Eccentric*," Lucy said. "The word was *eccentric*. But it doesn't mean weird exactly. Not exactly, but almost."

"I'm not eccentric!"

"Mum says it's because you live with just your dad. So maybe this girlfriend is a good thing, Bee. She'll stop you being eccentric and weird."

"I wasn't eccentric last term. You didn't mention anything then."

Sally and Lucy both looked at me. Sally put a hand on her hip, just like her mother did. "Maybe we've just realized it," she said.

"Lucy? You don't think I'm eccentric, do you?"

"I don't know that it's such a bad thing to be," Lucy said, but she didn't sound very sure about that.

I didn't want to be weird, but I didn't want Jazzi changing me, either.

"*You* are both getting weird," I said to Lucy and Sally. "That's what *I* think. I'm just me, the person I've always been."

"Not according to my mother," Sally said, and then the bell went, so I didn't find out exactly *what* Sally's mother thought of me.

"It's not that I don't like Jazzi," I told Nanna when she picked me up from school. "It's just that everything is different when she's around. She calls me Beatrice, too."

"Well, darling, that is your name, and a lovely one."

"It's an old-fashioned name, Nanna."

"Fashion, pff," and Nanna blew a raspberry into the air. "Who cares about fashion? It's a good name. It's got style."

"She cooked these scones but they weren't real scones. They didn't rise properly either. They were flat."

"The self-rising flour was probably old—your dad's pantry! It's a wonder she found any."

"Why are you taking her side, Nanna? You haven't even met her."

"I am not taking sides. I'm just giving the poor woman a chance."

We walked past the Star cinema and the expensive café and on to the bakery where Nanna ordered a coffee for herself and a hot chocolate for me. I was in for a talk. When she added yo-yo biscuits to the order, I knew it was a long talk. Sometimes these are good. She tells me about my mum and when I was a baby. Sometimes she gives me lectures about how I need to look after Dad, as if I were the grown-up, not him.

"You have to understand, Bee, that your dad has been a lonely man since Lindy died. We've all been lonely. God only knows how much I miss my girl. Children shouldn't be allowed to die first. It's cruel. But that's neither here nor there. Your father has sacrificed time and energy to raise you, Bee, but you're growing up, and now it's time for him to find companionship. This Jazzi sounds quite acceptable. It's a pity she doesn't have any children, but I don't suppose that can be helped."

"She doesn't like Fifi and Lulu much."

"Bee," Nanna said sternly, "you can't judge someone on whether or not they share your obsession with guinea pigs."

"I'm not obsessed," I said. "That's when you have posters and stuff on your wall. I have horses on my walls, not guinea pigs. I just like them, that's all. And they like me. It's good to own something that likes you, isn't it?"

"Well, that's probably how your dad feels about Jazzi—without the owning, of course. She likes him, obviously, or she wouldn't be staying the night and cooking scones! Nick needs someone to like him again."

"I don't just like Dad, I love him. Why don't I count?"

"Don't be ridiculous, Bee, of course you count. This is just different and I'm sure I don't have to spell out to you why. You're not a baby anymore. Good heavens, another couple of months and you'll be taller than I am."

"They were kissing in the kitchen. I saw them."

"How lovely for them—the kissing bit, I mean, not the being spied on bit."

"I wasn't spying, I just wanted a drink."

"Well, make sure you don't hang around them all the time. The last thing a new couple needs is some great girl poking her nose in where she shouldn't."

Honestly, Nanna was beginning to sound like one of those people on the radio who solve your problems for you. I didn't like being called a "great girl," either. It didn't mean what it normally meant, which was *wonderful* or even *marvelous*. It meant tall for my age and gangly. I knew by the way she said it. She said it that way when I bumped into her in the kitchen, too, when she was cooking. "Out of my way, you great girl!" and a whack on my bum if I didn't move fast enough.

"I think you should meet her before you decide you like her," I said crossly. "She wears very dark lipstick."

"I'll be meeting her today," Nanna said, sounding a little smug. "She's picking you up from my place today."

"But I can just walk home."

"I know that, but Jazzi wanted to collect you, and I didn't see anything wrong with it."

"I'm not a baby. I always walk home."

Sally and her mum walked past. I hoped they wouldn't see us but they did, and Sally's mum stopped to talk to Nanna.

"I hear Nick's got a girlfriend," was the first thing she said.

"He has," Nanna said, "and there are going to be a few teething problems." She looked at me as though I couldn't understand what she meant. I made a face but they were too busy talking to notice.

When we finally got home, Stan was already at Nanna's, pulling some weeds from around her front gate. He's lived next door to Nanna for the longest time. He has a crush on her. His eyes crinkle up when he sees her, he always carries her groceries in for her, and he calls her Patreeeecia.

Nanna gets all fluttery when he comes over, as if he doesn't visit her every day, and uses the blue and white willow plates. Dad calls them her romantic interest plates. Sometimes Stan brings around some of his homemade liqueur for after-dinner and they sit close together on the couch and argue about television programs and politics.

"Here are my girls," Stan said. "Patreeecia, time for a quick card game? What will it be, poker or blackjack?"

When Jazzi came around, I was winning at least two dollars in twenty-cent and ten-cent pieces, Stan was down to fifty cents, and Nanna claimed she was breaking even, but she was just as likely to have slipped a couple of fifty cents into her pocket when she refreshed the teapot.

"You open the door, Bee, you know her. Then you introduce her to me and Stan. Properly. The way I've taught you."

"Do I have to?"

"Bee!"

Jazzi's hair was pulled back into a frazzled ponytail, as though she were trying to look older than she really was. She still wore her plummy lipstick, though, and big earrings. She had a white shirt on, tucked into a denim skirt.

"Jazzi, this is my grandmother, I think she'd want you to call her Patricia. And this is Stan from next door. Nanna, Stan, I'd like you to meet Jazzi, Dad's girlfriend."

"Jazzi, how lovely to meet you. We're playing cards. We're inveterate gamblers around here. Stan's influence."

"Poker?" Jazzi said. "Oh, I like poker. Can you deal me in?"

I couldn't believe how quickly my two dollars disappeared.

"Jazzeee, you've got Lady Luck riding on your shoulder," Stan said, folding. "What a run of luck!"

"You've cleared me out. Time for a cup of tea?"

Jazzi left her winnings in the center of the table. "Do you have a jar or something?" she asked. "My dad always kept a jar of change so we could play again."

"We do too, dear. Nice of you to suggest it."

Jazzi got up and walked around the lounge room. "Is this you, Bee, and your mother?"

"Yes. That's when I was very little."

Jazzi peered at the photograph. "You look like your dad," she said, "except around the mouth and forehead, where you're just like her. She was beautiful, wasn't she?"

I looked at the photograph Jazzi held out. Everyone told me how much like Dad I looked, how I had his eyes. It worried me, having eyes like Dad. His sagged underneath in great baggy circles and the corners were a mass of fine crinkles. Dad's eyes had been like that ever since I could remember, and even in the photos of

19

his wedding they were starting to sag and he was quite young back then.

My mother's mouth was the kind supermodels have—full and curvy. I had never thought of my mouth before.

"See?" Jazzi traced her finger over my mother's mouth on a photograph just of her, taken way before she married my dad. "And here," she said, "your forehead, Beatrice, with your little widow's peak."

"Yes," Nanna said, coming up behind her, "you're quite right, Jazzi. I hadn't noticed how much Bee has changed in the last couple of years. She used to be the dead spit of Nick, but now she's much more like her mother. You're growing up, Bee, see, I told you so. It's lovely to hear you call her by her proper name, Jazzi. We've just all got lazy and now she's so used to Bee, she won't hear of us changing it back to what it should be."

"I like Bee. Mum called me Bee, you know."

"Your mum called you all sorts of things," Nanna said, putting her arm around my shoulders. "Mums always do. I heard her call you her little Beatrice many times when you were young. No, Bee was Nick's name for you, mostly. His little busy bee, the constant buzz buzz, he'd say. That was when you were babbling. That's what babies do when they're learning to talk. Lindy liked the joke and made you a skirt with bees on it. Do you remember that? I knitted a little green vest to go with it."

"You knit?" Jazzi asked.

"Oh, yes. It's back in fashion now, I believe. I've tried to teach Bee. She isn't as patient as she could be."

"I keep getting more stitches than I should have. It's not patience."

"Have you shown Jazzi your knitting? She's doing a scarf. I don't know why we always start with scarves, singularly boring if you ask me."

"Everyone's wearing them," I said, "and Lucy and Sal thought it was cool."

"You'll have to show me, Beatrice. I had no idea!"

For the next hour I watched Nanna bring out photos and samples of her own knitting. Jazzi exclaimed over them, even the boring ones. I sat and yawned loudly on the couch, hoping they'd notice me.

I missed my favorite television show because Nanna wouldn't let me have the television on when there was a guest. By the time Jazzi was ready to go, I was grumpy.

"I really like Patricia," Jazzi said later to my dad. "All that knitting, and it's quite beautiful. Really crafted, Nick. None of this kind of flash stuff we're all doing, relying on novelty yarns, but great craftwork. And she's a lot of fun. They were playing poker with the next-door neighbor when I arrived. He's obviously crazy about her. I had the best afternoon!"

"I had the worst afternoon," I said, pushing Thai chicken salad with lime and chili dressing around my

21

plate. I didn't like the little green leaves under the chicken or the beans or the snow peas. They all tasted too green. When I tried to explain that to Jazzi and Dad, they just looked exasperated. "I lost at poker and I had to miss *Pony School* and *Feral Felines and Crazy Canines* because Nanna and Jazzi were talking about boring old knitting. It's always either kissing or knitting around here."

Dad shot me The Look and then actually shifted his chair a little so he was facing Jazzi square on and could only look at me sideways. It was so rude I didn't bother showing Jazzi my scarf and I went to bed very early without being told, but no one even noticed that.

The guinea pig letters

*A*s it turned out, Jazzi's idea of cleaning out the guinea pig hutch myself wasn't all that bad. Jazzi was at our place more and more and cleaning up after Fifi and Lulu gave me something to do while she and Dad gazed into each other's eyes, held hands, and drank endless cups of tea. At least with Jazzi around so much, the guinea pigs never ran out of apples or celery or broccoli.

Fifi and Lulu began to come out of their little bedroom when they heard me coming. I would squat down next to the hutch and hold out bits of food without moving, even though sometimes my legs began to hurt. Eventually Fifi, she was the brave one, would dart forward and grab the celery or apple or broccoli and then rush away and nibble at it down in the far corner. Once she'd done it, Lulu would come in twitching and nervy to get the other piece.

But there were other ideas of Jazzi's that weren't so good.

"Why do I have to make my bed in the morning?"

"Because it looks neat and pretty."

"I don't have time in the morning."

"Get up a little earlier. It only takes five minutes."

"Five minutes when I could be asleep and dreaming."

"Or five minutes when you could be up, enjoying the day."

"I'd rather enjoy my dreams."

"Why do you always have to argue?"

"I don't always argue. It's just that I do prefer dreaming. Once the morning starts it's just go, go, go and everyone ends up grumpy."

"I just want you to make your bed. It's not much to ask."

"I didn't have to do it for Dad."

"But you do have to for me."

"It seems like I have to do a lot of things for you when you don't even live here and we're not even related. I don't think it's fair. You're not my mother, Jazzi, and you never will be."

Jazzi stopped making my lunch sandwiches and just looked at me. I swallowed hard. I didn't like the way she was looking. I didn't mind it if she got mad, but she didn't look angry; she just looked very sad. Her eyes went all wavery the way mine did right before I started to cry. She sniffed, turned away, and did something in the sink. When she turned back her eyes were okay again and I thought I must have been imagining things.

"I know I'm not your mother. I'm not stupid enough to think I can replace her in either your life or your dad's."

"I don't like how everything's changed," I said. "I liked things the way they were, before you came along and ruined everything."

I called good-bye to Dad and walked to school with Jazzi without talking once. She pointed out things on the way like she always did—a puppy in a car window, a baby so new its face was still all crumpled, and some bright pink flowers on a bush—but I didn't even look at them.

Jazzi worked five mornings a week at the high school up the road as a Special Education aide.

"Which is terrific," Dad said, "because it means that she'll be able to drop you off at school some mornings and then some afternoons she'll pick you up and some afternoons Nanna will pick you up."

As it turned out, Nanna hardly ever picked me up. Some afternoons I used to walk over to her place because I missed her. Then we'd all sit around playing cards just like we used to. Often, though, Jazzi had things she wanted me to do.

Some of these were okay. If it was hot, we'd go swimming at the pool across the road. Nanna didn't like going to the pool, because she had to sit out on the grass or in the sun and she said she was too old to do that. Jazzi didn't mind. She'd bring her knitting or a book and a big hat and sit there wrapped up in a sarong. Sometimes she came and did some laps of breaststroke, holding her head high out of the water.

Other things weren't good.

"Let me see that project, Beatrice. That looks quite exciting. Japanese culture is very interesting and very different from our own. We'll walk up to the library together and see what books we can find. Look, Bee, you can do a whole section on cooking. That will be fun." Sometimes it felt to me as though Jazzi actually enjoyed my homework.

When she had things she had to do, she'd tell me to go and see what Fifi and Lulu were up to.

It was one of those afternoons that I found the envelope. It was stuck through the cage, but high up.

Lulu pointed it out to me. She was standing on her hind legs, sniffing at it. It was a tiny little envelope with *Bee* written on it in gold pen.

I sat down on the hay bale and opened it. Glitter fell on my lap and skirt and then an eensy little folded-up piece of paper.

"Curiouser and curiouser," I said to Lulu and Fifi, who were both squeaking and darting around. And then, because even guinea pigs like to know things, I said, "That's from *Alice in Wonderland*. You'd like that book because it has a rabbit in it."

I unfolded the note. It said:

Dear Bee,
Thank you for the celery, apple, and broccoli and for cleaning out the cage so beautifully. We like it when you read to us, too. Wind in the Willows was good, but the Wild Wood was scary.
Love,
Lulu and Fifi

It took me a while to read it even though it was quite short. The printed letters were very small.

I had a stationery set from my last birthday which I'd never used because I had no one to write to. The paper had daisies on it and I thought the guineas would like that. I cut a sheet in quarters very carefully, ruling the lines first. I practiced making my writing small enough on scrap paper.

Dear Lulu and Fifi,

What is it like having fur on all the time? Would you like a bath? I asked Jazzi if I could bathe you but she said you might be frightened and that it would have to be a very very hot day. I have an old baby bath and you could both swim around. I bet Dad would let me do that sometime.

Love,

Bee

"The guinea pigs wrote me a note today," I told Dad as soon as he got home from work, "so after dinner I'm making a special postbox. Then we can post letters to each other in the box and they won't be tempted to eat them."

"That's a good idea," Dad said.

"What a lovely imagination." Jazzi smiled. "Do you want any help making it?"

"No thanks, Jazzi. Dad, did you hear me? I said that after tea I'd put my letter for the guineas in their new postbox."

"I heard, Bee. Very nice. I'm sure they'll appreciate that. Jazzi's offered to help, too. I must say, Jazzi, another delicious meal. Thank you. What did we do before Jazzi, Bee?"

"We had pizza," I said, "and noodles and chicken in plum sauce. Nanna made casseroles sometimes and soup in winter and we had barbecues, too. I was planning to learn to cook."

"I'm sure Jazzi would teach you to cook, Bee, if you asked her nicely."

"It doesn't matter anymore because Jazzi cooks all the time."

"Oh, I'd love to teach you. Maybe after dinner we could think about something to cook for tomorrow night."

"Are you going to be here tomorrow night as well?" I didn't mean the words to sound as horrible as they did, and I bit my lip as soon as they'd left my mouth, but it didn't help. Dad looked furious, and Jazzi was flustered.

"I just thought—"

"That's enough, Bee."

"Anyway, I'm doing the postbox for Fifi and—"

"I said, that's enough. I don't think we're interested in what such a rude girl has to say."

"I didn't mean it," I muttered, but it was too late and I didn't get any ice cream.

I made the postbox though. I wrote *POSTBOX* on it in large letters and wired it to the outside of their cage.

I stayed in the cubbyhouse until it was quite dark, hoping that Dad would come out to see where I was and what I was up to, but in the end I gave up because the tree ferns made scary tapping noises on the cubby roof and it seemed sensible to go inside where the lights were on.

Harley and To Be

When Jazzi picked me up from school later that week she wasn't smiling.

"Beatrice, come on, hurry up. We've got to go somewhere."

"I'm thirsty."

"We haven't got time for this; come on."

When I rush something, my fingers and feet seem to get bigger and it's hard not to fumble and stumble. I tried to pull the zipper up on my backpack but it got stuck, so I just threw it over one shoulder and ran after Jazzi, who was marching off, her little heels clip-clopping quickly.

"I'm thirsty," I said again, catching up. "We had

running before and Mrs. P. wouldn't let anyone get a drink afterward. She's so mean."

"You can get something later," Jazzi said, turning back to look at me. And then, "Oh, you silly girl, Beatrice, you're spilling everything."

"I need a new backpack," I told her as we picked everything up. "I think this one is broken."

"It's not broken; you've jammed something in the zipper. Here, what's all this?" Jazzi yanked at my scarf.

"That's my knitting!" I said. "Don't touch that!"

"But it's caught, Beatrice. Look."

Sure enough, there was a piece of my special fat chunky yarn stuck between the zipper teeth.

"Oh no," I wailed. "It's really ruined now."

"You'll get it out," Jazzi said, grabbing my hand, "but later, okay? Right now we have to hurry."

"It's taken me ages," I said, "all that knitting. It's a bit weird, I know, but it was my first go and you can muck up your first go. Why are we in such a hurry?"

She didn't answer, just pushed me along to her car. It might have been clean, but that didn't mean it started any more easily.

"I'm really thirsty," I told Jazzi again, in case she'd forgotten. "We did running this afternoon and then Sam pushed Andrew and Andrew flicked water at him and we weren't allowed—"

"Bee, just shut up, will you! I'm trying to make this car start."

I was so shocked that Jazzi had called me by my right name that I shut my mouth straightaway and swallowed the rest of my sentence.

"Come on," Jazzi muttered at the car, "please work." She tried the key again and the car made a hopeful coughing sound that died away almost immediately.

"I think you've flooded it," I said, forgetting to keep my mouth shut. "Nanna does that sometimes in winter. Her car doesn't like the cold."

Jazzi looked at me and I thought she was going to shout again. Instead she took such a deep breath I could hear it go all the way down to her tummy.

"I think you're right, Beatrice," she said. "I think that's exactly what I've done. Okay, that's okay. Why don't you just run up to that shop and get us two juices while we wait for this old car to work?"

She handed me ten dollars.

"I don't suppose you're hungry, too?" I asked.

"Something to eat, too—something salty," Jazzi said, "for both of us. But nothing with chicken flavor."

"I hate chicken flavor."

"Well, we've got something in common then." Jazzi smiled a small, sad smile.

When I got back, the car was humming away, Jazzi

had new lipstick on, and her nose was all flaky looking because she'd powdered it.

"I didn't know whether to get one bag or two," I told her, "but I thought it would be safer if you were driving to get two."

"Just don't get crumbs everywhere," she answered, "and don't wipe your hands on the seat."

"So where are we going?" I asked finally as we drove through streets that were only half-familiar.

"To see my brother." Jazzi dove her hand into the chip bag.

"You don't have a brother."

"Yes, I do," Jazzi said, tipping the chip bag up and shaking them straight out into her mouth while someone behind us honked because the lights had just turned green. "Shut up, you road pig!" she shouted at the rear-vision mirror.

I was beginning to enjoy the drive. Unexpected things were happening.

"You've never told us. Does Dad know?"

Jazzi sighed and turned down a little street. I recognized it. Dad and I used to go sometimes to the adventure playground there. Jazzi stopped the car right opposite the playground but I didn't think we were going there.

"No," she said, "your dad doesn't know and I don't want you to tell him, Beatrice."

"Why?"

"Harley's not like . . . he's got problems, Beatrice. He's always had problems. You know how some people are born with blue eyes and some with brown? Well, Harley was born with a different kind of brain."

"What sort of brain?"

"Just different. His brain's wired differently."

"Wired differently?" Jazzi was making less and less sense.

"Look Beatrice, don't you have anyone in your class at school who is, you know, a bit different?"

"Rebecca J.'s little brother Nat is different. He's acoustic."

"Acoustic?" Jazzi repeated.

The word didn't sound right to me either.

"*Acoustic* means not electric," Jazzi said. "Do you mean *autistic*?"

"Probably," I said. "They have to lock the kitchen cupboards at night and there are wind chimes above his door so his parents will wake up if he leaves his room at night. I'd like some wind chimes, but not above my door—outside my window. Rebecca says that he shouts a lot, too, and doesn't even know why you cry if he hurts you."

"Harley isn't exactly autistic, but he does shout sometimes and he doesn't know that he hurts other people, either. Look Beatrice, I really didn't want to bring

35

you with me today but I have to see him every week.
Don't you worry about anything, though. You just sit
quietly, be a good girl, and don't worry. Harley lives with
a couple of other people a bit like him, but no one will
hurt you, no matter how strangely they behave. Okay?"

"Sure." I shrugged. She seemed to be making a big
fuss about nothing.

We drove off a little way and then stopped in front of
an ordinary house. Two big velvet lounge chairs were
sitting out on the front lawn with a little white table
between them. A man sat in one of the chairs. He had a
big beach towel over his face. A woman was in the other,
jabbing her fingers at the air as she talked to the towel.

Jazzi checked her lipstick in the mirror and gave
a practice smile. "Let's go," she said and smiled again,
showing her teeth. She reached over to the backseat and
picked up two bags containing sticky buns. "He likes
these," she said, "but you never know whether it will be
the apple or the pink icing. I always get both."

"Do you think we could have some of the one he
doesn't want?"

"Probably. Sometimes he likes to keep both. It just
depends what kind of mood he's in. Follow me and don't
pay any attention to anything anyone says, okay?"

The woman in the green velvet chair was sitting bolt
upright now and watched us as we pushed open the
gate and went up the stairs.

"Hello!" Jazzi made the word dance up and down and she waved her fingers at the woman. "Just visiting Harley."

"He's inside. Plotting," the woman said and then suddenly bellowed, her voice sounding too big for her body, "Harley! The woman who says she's your sister is here again with another one. A smaller one."

Jazzi went up the stairs but the woman kept staring at me. It would have been rude of me to say nothing, so I said, "Hi, I'm Bee. Short for Beatrice."

"Buzz buzz," the woman said. "The flower woman's here with a little insect," and she cackled loudly, sounding just like a witch.

I hurried after Jazzi. "Why are you the flower woman?"

"Shh." Jazzi tried the buzzer and listened. Nothing happened. She rapped loudly on the glass panels. The door opened quickly, as though someone had been waiting behind it.

Harley was standing where we couldn't quite see all of him, behind the door, which had kind of closed back on him when it opened for us. I jumped when he stuck his head around a little.

"You shouldn't do that, Harley," Jazzi said. "You frighten people."

"People frighten me," Harley said. "Who is this, Jasmine?"

I stared at Jazzi—*Jasmine*? "Jasmine?" I squeaked.

"She doesn't even know you." Harley's voice came from behind the door now, which he'd pulled shut on himself.

"Do come out, Harley," *Jasmine* said. "I've bought you some sticky buns."

"Which one do you like today?" I asked, poking my head around the door a little. "We bought both, apple and pink icing." It was like watching Fifi and Lulu. First he kind of hunched down, as though he was trying to hide. I stayed exactly where I was and made myself as still as I could be, the way I was with the guinea pigs. "I like apple," I said after a while, just to make conversation, "and I particularly like the apple with walnuts. My name's Bee." I didn't offer him my hand to shake because I couldn't remember which hand to hold out and also I didn't want to startle him.

"To be or not to be." He leaned forward so his head was quite close to mine. "The question, little Bee, are you or are you not?"

"I am," I said, "or I wouldn't be here, would I?"

"I don't know. Sometimes I am here and sometimes I go away for a time. Time itself is quite slippery. Pink icing. Today is a pink icing day because the sky is so blue. You and Jasmine can have the apple." And all of Harley emerged from behind the door.

He was taller than Jazzi but you'd know straightaway they were brother and sister, just the way I could tell that Uncle Rob was Mum's brother when I looked at her photo next to his.

Harley had the same shaped face and eyes, the same slightly too big mouth and surprised eyebrows, but his eyes were all puffy and there was a not-quite beard growing on his chin. Even though he looked old, he seemed young.

He put the pink icing bun on a little plate, not worried that most of the bun hung over the sides of the plate. Jazzi sat down and folded her hands in her lap.

"You could share it with the others," she suggested. "You could call Bill and Laura in for tea and sticky buns, Harley."

Harley shook his head. "Laura's making holes in the air," he said, imitating Laura's jabbing finger. "I don't like it when she does that, and Bill's hiding."

"Are you taking your pills?" Jazzi asked very quietly. "Has Tony dropped around?"

"Yes, yes, yes." Harley stuffed a big pulled-off piece of bun in his mouth and didn't look at Jazzi. "Tea?" he asked, spraying crumbs everywhere.

"That would be lovely." Jazzi's hands were still folded, and her piece of bun, torn off by Harley, lay untouched on her plate.

"Tea, To Be? A nice cup of tea for Bee? Tea, bee, tree, bee, true bee, two bee?"

"Thanks."

"Then we'll have to go," Jazzi said.

"You just got here," Harley said, his voice flat and cold. "Jasmine is always rushing, rush rush rush. I bet the True Bee doesn't rush rush rush."

"I hate rushing." I felt sorry for him. The corners of his mouth were drooped and he looked like a sad puppy. "I hate it when you have to hurry up, get ready, and forget things. They always say it's your fault, but it isn't really. It's the clock's fault."

"True Bee, To Bee, has theys too?" Harley's question made no sense to me.

"Harley, Bee's a child. She's Nick's daughter. Do you remember, I told you I was going out with Nick? My boyfriend? I showed you his photo. Do you remember his photo?"

"He looked worried." Harley nodded. "Worried, anxious, nervous, confused, confounded, distressed. Tick all or none of the above."

"He had the sun in his eyes," Jazzi said, her voice sharp as a smack.

"He always looks like that," I told Harley at more or less the same time.

He turned his head quickly, looking at Jazzi first, then me. Watching him made me feel dizzy.

"Which is it—sun or always? Always or sun? Nervous, confounded, world too much for him sensitive kind of guy, or just the sun squinting his eyes shut. Which is it?"

"The sun," Jazzi said firmly. "Nick's a very solid kind of person, Harley. He works in the public service."

"Aha, a servant of the public. But where is the public? Who is public, who is private? I'm a private kind of person. Where do I get a servant from, hmm? Do the private get servants, too? Do they, To Be? Does your dad work as a private or just a public servant? Public and private, sun and worry. Things happen in pairs."

Harley started to make three cups of tea with the one tea bag as he was talking. I didn't like tea much but it took him such a long time to make the tea, filling the cups up with exactly the right amount of water, pouring in a little milk, measuring the sugar and then dancing the tea bag around in the cups before squeezing it out gently, that I couldn't refuse the cup he finally offered to me.

"Can't spare more tea bags," he said. "They count them, you know." He jerked his head toward the front door which still swung open. "They count everything—squeezes of toothpaste, bristles in the brushes, teeth in the comb, soapsuds, dishes in the sink, tea bags, plastic bags, empty wrappers, biscuits in the barrel. You should get a job counting, I told them, but what could they count? What could they count, Bee?"

"I don't know." I couldn't think of anything, and then I thought of those signs outside parking places, 226 spaces upstairs. "Empty parking lots," I said, "for shopping centers and special events."

"You can bring her all the time," Harley told Jazzi, holding her slightly away from him as she tried to hug him good-bye. "She's all right. I like her. She doesn't work for them, she's too small, and she doesn't care what bun she eats. Jasmine, you will bring her again, I like her."

I looked from Harley's big grin to Jazzi's pale face and stepped forward. "I like you, too, Harley," I said and nearly offered him my left hand—I had remembered!— but didn't at the last minute, in case he got scared.

"I don't see why you don't tell Dad," I said on the way home. "He'll like Harley. Harley will like him. They'll get on. Dad gets on with everyone. He's laid-back." Uncle Rob's phrase didn't sound as right when I said it.

"Harley was good today." Jazzi smiled a small, tight smile as though it was all she could afford at that moment. "I think that was partly you. He liked you. He often doesn't like people. It takes him a while to realize it, but in the end he doesn't like them and sometimes he tells them that and they feel—"

"Sad?"

"Sad, angry, whatever." Now Jazzi sounded a little like Harley but more sarcastic, but I decided not to tell her that.

"The people he lives with are pretty weird," I said instead. "Maybe he should live somewhere else—your place. Why doesn't he live with you, Jazzi—oops, I mean, *Jasmine*."

"I am not Jasmine!" Jazzi hurtled through a yellow light. "I'm Jazzi. And Harley can't live with me. He can't even remember not to call me Jasmine, but that's not the reason. He's not stable. He's not actually normal. He's just as weird as the people he lives with and he needs to live with people like him. He's out of control. You're too young, Beatrice, to understand . . ."

"Bee," I said. "Jasmine—Jazzi. Beatrice—Bee. If you'd just remember that we'd get along a lot better, I reckon."

There was complete silence until we drove up outside our house, and then Jazzi turned to me. She'd bitten all her brave lipstick off so her mouth was nearly the same color as the rest of her face.

"It's a shame," she said softly. "I just wanted to call you by the name your parents gave you. It's such a good name—strong and passionate, but gentle. I thought of how your mother might like you called by your whole, complete name. But it doesn't matter, I suppose, Bee. Let's have pizza for dinner, okay?"

When I got up the next morning, my scarf had been coaxed out of the zipper and was carefully rolled up beside my school backpack. Neither Jazzi nor I mentioned Harley to Dad.

Nuclear families

WOOF

"So you've got a stepmum now?" Sally said at lunch-time. "Is she nice?"

"Jazzi's not my stepmum."

"Well, she's picked you up every afternoon this week, so that means she must be living at your place, and that means she's your stepmum."

"She doesn't live with us. She's got a flat all of her own. She just visits. She's my dad's girlfriend."

"She'll be your stepmum soon," Lucy butted in. "That's what happens."

"I don't want a stepmum."

"Well, you need one, that's what my mum says."

"I don't need one. Dad and me, we're fine. We've got each other and Nanna. And we see Uncle Rob and Aunty Maree."

"And Jazzi now," Sally said, nudging Lucy with her elbow. "You guys see a lot of Jazzi."

"Well, they have to," Lucy said. "She's going to be Bee's stepmum, so of course they see a lot of her."

"She isn't going to be my stepmum. She doesn't even live with us. Will you stop being mean?"

"It'll be good," Sally said. "You'll be like a proper family again."

"We are already," I said. I could feel tears stinging behind my eyes. "Dad and I are a proper family."

"Well, you're not a nuclear family and that's what you should be. Nuclear families have a mother and a father and something else, but I've forgotten the other thing . . ."

"A dog?" Lucy asked. "I think a proper family should have a dog."

"I don't think Dad said anything about a dog." Sally sounded uncertain. "But I remember the mum and dad bit."

"We were nuclear but then we became different. It's not our fault. Lots of people don't live with their dad and their mum. What about Josh and Sam?"

"They see their dads on weekends," Lucy said. "And anyway Sam has a stepdad."

"He's cool, too," Sally said. "He gives Sam great presents all the time and he plays footie."

"Jazzi's okay," I said. "She can knit."

"So?"

"Sally, you wanted to learn to knit when I started. You said you did. You said my scarf was cool."

"It's too hot to wear a scarf anyway."

"It won't be by the time I finish it."

Sally shrugged. "We don't want to be your best friends anymore," she said. "You don't tell the truth about things."

"I do so." I looked at Lucy. "You want to be best friends, don't you, Lucy?"

Lucy didn't look at me. She was busy taking everything out of her lunch box and putting it on her lap.

"Lucy, you know what we agreed on," Sally said, kicking Lucy with her foot.

Lucy's head bobbed up and down but she didn't say anything and she didn't look up.

"So there, Bee, we can't be best friends with a liar."

"What have I lied about?"

"If you don't know, we're not going to tell you."

"That's not fair. I haven't lied. I know I haven't lied."

"What about the guinea pig letters?" Lucy said softly, still examining her lunch with enormous concentration. "We all know that guinea pigs can't write."

"I didn't say they wrote them. I said my dad probably did, but that it was fun pretending."

"You told us that Lulu and Fifi wrote you letters," Sally said, "and you told us that you could knit, and you told us that Jazzi wasn't your stepmum. That's three lies, Bee."

"I can knit."

"Your scarf looks demented. It starts off small and then gets bigger and bigger in the middle."

"That's because I keep picking up stitches," I said miserably. "Nanna says I'll get better. And Jazzi's not my stepmum."

"She will be, though," Sally said, "so it counts as a lie."

"You don't know that. You can't say that, Sally Nixon. You've got no right." I stood up, thinking I'd have to get away before I cried in front of them, and bent down to pick up my lunch box. Sally deliberately kicked it with her foot so my sandwich spilled out on to the ground.

"Sorry," she said, looking up at me. "I didn't mean to."

I looked at the perfectly straight part that divided her head and her hair into two neat plaits. I bent down, grabbed one of her plaits and yanked hard. "Oops, sorry," I said. "I didn't mean to." And I pulled harder with each word.

I heard her wailing behind me, when I was halfway across the playground. I hadn't even made it to the library before Sally, Lucy, and Mrs. Petrovsky caught up with me. Sally's face was all streaky with tears and even her freckles looked pink.

"Is this true, Beatrice?" Mrs. Petrovsky asked me, taking hold of both my hands as though she would know from the feel of them whether I'd pulled Sally's hair.

"Yes," I muttered, looking at her shoes. They were dusty from the playground.

"Why, Beatrice?"

"Because she said I didn't come from a proper family."

"I didn't," Sal hiccuped. "I said she'd be happy when she got a stepmum, Mrs. P., that's all."

"Anyway," I said, looking at Sal's pink streaky face, "her part is too straight."

"That's not a good reason for physical violence, Beatrice. Who is coming to collect you today?"

"Jazzi."

"I'll make sure I have a word with her, and in the meantime you can apologize to Sally and stay on yard duty with me and help me pick up the rubbish."

"Yes, Mrs. P."

Jazzi wasn't impressed when she came out of the classroom.

"No, I quite understand," I heard her saying. "Of course, I'll be sure to explain to her father . . . It's a delicate time for us all . . . Difficult, you know, particularly when . . . But thank you. Yes, thank you."

We walked out of the school yard in silence.

"Well, Beatrice," Jazzi said finally when we were halfway up the hill to home, "I must say I'm surprised."

"It wasn't my fault."

"Pulling someone's plaits not once but four or five times is hardly an accident, Beatrice."

"You sound like a teacher."

"What am I going to tell your father?"

"I don't care."

"Well, I care. I want to know what I'm to tell him."

"That Sally and Lucy were mean. I got into trouble at school. I had to pick up papers all lunchtime, too. My desk got moved to the front. I don't know if I'll ever get back to where I used to be. Nothing happened to Sally and she was horrid."

"What did she do?" Jazzi asked. "Bee? What did she do? I want to hear your side of the story, too, you know."

But I couldn't tell her, so we walked home in silence.

At home she tried again, making a cup of herbal tea for herself and pouring me a glass of water from the fridge, which was better than juice, she said, because it actually quenched your thirst. We both sat down at the kitchen table and ate half a Muesli bar each.

"So," she said after a while, "Sally was mean. What did she say?"

"That she and Lucy didn't want to be best friends with me anymore because I told lies."

"Lies about what?"

"Just stuff."

"That's not a good answer, Beatrice."

How could I tell her? It sounded as though I didn't want her as a stepmum, and it was true, I didn't, but I still couldn't tell her. I looked at her watching me. I knew when she got up in the morning she always put mascara and eyeliner on and that she had a special little brush to brush her eyebrows. That had always struck me as being strange, but now, looking at her little surprised eyebrows, I realized how thin they were and how, if there was even one hair out of place, they'd look crazy. No wonder she brushed them.

"I don't know," I muttered. "They were just being mean."

"Beatrice, this is your last chance. If you can't tell me the whole story, I shall simply have to report what I know to your father and let him deal with it."

"I don't care."

Dad didn't do more than grunt at me when she told him.

"Flash in the pan," he said, sweeping it all away with his arm. "Girls, they're always doing this kind of thing, aren't you, Bee? You must remember that, Jazzi, from your days at school."

"No, I don't, Nick," Jazzi said in a tight little voice. "I certainly didn't pull anyone's plaits three or four times."

"I'm sure she didn't pull hard. Bee, you wouldn't have pulled Sally's hair hard, darling?"

I thought of how I'd seen the hair strain against the clean skin of Sally's parting. How hard was hard? I decided it was having hairs come out in your hand. "No, not really," I said.

"It'll blow over," Dad said. "The important thing is that we're all here having a lovely dinner—another lovely dinner, thanks to Jazzi."

After I'd gone to bed, Jazzi came into my room and sat down on the end of my bed, without me even inviting her to.

"You know," she said, "in my experience, things between friends need to be sorted out. If I can help at all, Beatrice, I'd be happy to. I'm very fond of you, and your dad, of course. You do know that, don't you?"

"But you're not my stepmum," I said quickly, "are you? I mean, for you to be my stepmum you'd have to live here, and you don't. You've got a flat and you live there."

"Well, yes, that's true. No, I'm not your stepmother, Beatrice, but I hope you think of me as a friend, nonetheless." She looked sad when she said that.

"I just want to know," I said, "that's all."

"Is that what the girls said you were lying about? Did you call me your stepmum and they said I wasn't?"

"Something like that." I couldn't tell her the truth.

"Oh, Bee, I think the intention is just as important as where someone lives. I want to look after you like a stepmother would. You're very important to me. Don't you worry about what the girls said. I'm sure your dad's right, and that it will all blow over."

She offered to tuck me in after that, but I was tucked in already so I couldn't see the point. She smoothed my hair back off my face and I thought she would have liked to have kissed me good night but I rolled over before she had a chance. I didn't mind her getting the story wrong but I didn't want to encourage too much stepmotherly behavior.

Just before I went to sleep I thought of what I should have said to Sally. I should have asked her if she thought the nuclear bomb was a good thing. Then I should have said that if the nuclear bomb was such a bad thing, what made nuclear families so good? Didn't it just mean that they'd blow up too, like the bomb?

I didn't have a chance to tell Sally that because neither she nor Lucy talked to me for the rest of the week and I had to tag along after the teacher on yard duty and play Pick Up Papers. I couldn't wait for the whole thing to blow over but it looked as though it was going to hang around for a while.

The Jazzi-free weekend

I stayed with Nanna on the weekend because Dad and Jazzi wanted to go away. I suggested they take me too, but Dad laughed and tugged my hair and said that wouldn't be the most romantic thing now would it? They wanted some child-free time, he said, not that I wasn't the best girl in the world but he and Jazzi wanted to go out for dinner and tell each other soppy things over a glass or two of champagne.

I told him that I didn't mind, but asked if he and I could have a Jazzi-free weekend sometime, too. I reminded him that I hardly ever seemed to see him by himself these days, and although Jazzi might be wonderful I wanted to do some of the things Dad and I used to do together, before Jazzi.

"It seems fair," I said, "if you and Jazzi can go away without me, that you and I can stay home without her."

"Well, yes, I suppose so, Bee. But let's not put it to Jazzi quite like that, okay? She might be hurt."

"You put it to me like that," I said.

"But I've known you all your life," Dad said, "and I can trust you to understand and not be hurt. You're a sensible kid, Bee. You know that adults need time away together and that I love you and always will and that has nothing to do with Jazzi and me."

I didn't feel sensible. I felt hurt but I couldn't tell Dad that.

"Where are you going?"

"Daylesford," Dad said. "It's got everything—good restaurants, some shops that Jazzi will love, and I'll book a spa for us, too. The water is supposed to have special healing properties. I think Jazzi would like that, don't you?"

"I guess so. Is it the beach?"

"Good heavens no, it's the mountains."

I felt better then. I wouldn't have been able to be sensible about the beach.

In the end I had a good weekend anyway. I beat Nanna and Stan at poker and won seven dollars and eighty-five cents. We went to see a movie together and to the Jade Cherry Blossom for dinner.

"Makes a change," Nanna said.

"Not as spicy as Thai," Stan said. "I think I'll have sweet and sour pork."

"Jazzi doesn't like Chinese food," I said. "She said it's got too much MG something in it and that they use too much food coloring to make things look red and shiny."

"Ssh, Bee."

"Sorry." I thought I'd whispered quietly, but Nanna looked around worriedly in case someone had heard me. They hadn't though, because they brought us over free prawn crackers. That could have been because of Stan. He always ate there on movie night. He had pizza or pasta at Bella Mama's on Tuesdays, the Polish Club on Thursdays, his own cabbage soup on Fridays, and the rest of the time Nanna took pity on him.

"I enjoy a multicultural diet," he told me once. "In this beautiful country of ours, I can eat a different nationality every night of the week."

"So where were your dad and his girlfriend going again?" Stan asked.

"Daylesford," I told him. "It's in the mountains."

"Ah, Daylesford. They will be enjoying a romantic spa together. It is a beautiful place. I should take your Nanna there. What do you say, Patreeecia? We deserve a romantic weekend, too."

"Oh, Stan, at our age. What a suggestion!"

"Well, if not at our age, when? Soon we'll be dead, Patreeecia. That's what happens at our age."

"You're not that old," I said, "either of you." But secretly I thought even Dad was a bit too old for a romantic weekend.

"I think we should do more at our age." Stan reached across the table and grabbed Nanna's hand. "It is nice at our age to do unexpected, pleasurable things. There are some things you should never be too old to do. Like a spa, for example. It would be good for our arthritis."

"You get these essential oils put in them," I told him. "They probably have something for arthritis."

"There you are. Bee agrees with me."

"Oh, Stan." But Nanna didn't take her hand away, I noticed, and Stan held it until our meal arrived.

I meant to ask Nanna if that meant she was Stan's girlfriend, but I forgot because we didn't get home until late.

When Dad got back from Daylesford I told him he should give all his Daylesford brochures to Stan, so that he and Nanna could chose somewhere to stay. Dad looked a bit surprised, so I didn't tell him about the hand-holding at the Jade Cherry Blossom. He and Jazzi brought me back a bead bracelet from Daylesford and Jazzi had some wool she'd bought there.

"For a vest for your dad," she said. "It has to be a vest, not a sweater."

"Why?"

"Because of the Boyfriend Sweater Curse." She laughed, but she looked hard at Dad when she said it.

"The what?"

"Knitting wisdom says that as soon as you make a sweater for a boyfriend, the relationship breaks up."

"That's just not going to happen," Dad said, hugging her.

"That's right—because I'm not making a sweater. I'm making a vest."

"Why would someone dump you for making them a sweater?"

"You should see some of those sweaters," Dad joked, keeping one arm around Jazzi. "But not my chocolate vest—it will be the envy of the office."

"So has that happened to you?" I asked Jazzi.

"No, but I've never knitted a boyfriend a sweater."

"Because of the curse?"

"Well, you have to like someone an awful lot to make a sweater for them."

"What about husbands? Is there a husband sweater curse? And what about Stan and Nanna? She's making him a sweater."

"Husbands are different," Jazzi said, "and Stan's different too. He wouldn't dump your Nanna."

"So you can make a husband a sweater?"

"Of course."

"How come?"

"Because . . . well, I suppose because once you're married to someone . . . well, I don't know, Beatrice, I've never been married. Ask your dad."

"I don't know anything about knitting," Dad said, "but I do know there's ice cream in the freezer for anyone who wants dessert."

"Is there a girlfriend sweater curse?" I asked. This cursing thing was getting to me. I wanted to know.

"What?"

"Well, suppose I knitted something for Sally or Lucy, not that I would because we're not talking anymore, but if we were and I did, then would she dump me as a friend? Or suppose I was going out with a guy who knitted . . . I mean, I don't know that any guys do, but if they did and I was with one and he knitted me a sweater, a really cool sweater in my favorite colors, would I dump him? And if you dump someone when they've knitted you something, do you have to give it back?"

"Bee, I think this is taking an odd little superstition just a bit far, okay?" Dad said.

"There are some knitters," Jazzi said, "that get their boyfriends to sign contracts before they start knitting a sweater."

"Contracts?"

"Mmm. So, for example, I'd get your dad to sign a contract stating that if he dumped . . . I mean, if the relationship between us ended, say, up to six months after the sweater was finished, I'd get to keep the sweater. He'd have to give it back."

"You're making this up," Dad said, laughing.

"No, Nick, it's true. Why not? Think of the time and effort that gets put into something like a man's sweater. The yarn alone—well, the yarn for your vest wasn't exactly cheap. If you spend time making something, you want it to be the best possible thing you can make, don't you? You don't want to skimp on the yarn or do a second-rate design. You want it to be a work of art. It should be a work of art. Something you can hand over with pride and something the other person can wear with pride."

"It's only knitting." Dad smiled. "I mean, it's not Michelangelo's ceiling or anything. It's just a sweater."

I thought for a minute I could see tears coming into Jazzi's eyes, but she turned away from us before I could be certain and busied herself in the cutlery drawer, getting ice cream spoons. When she turned back, she wore a half-smile on her face.

"Perhaps knitting is as close as you can get to the Sistine Chapel. Perhaps knitting is your way of expressing, not just love for the recipient of the knitting but love of color, texture, and pattern. And you know you're not Michelangelo, because you failed art because the art teacher was some ghastly woman who thought you should be more like your . . . well, someone else, and you weren't, but you were good with some things, and color and patterns were those things. So what you do with your knitting is as important to you as Michelangelo's chapel was to him. I'd want a contract to get back that knitting."

"Well, yes," Dad said, "I'm sure you would. And I'd be happy to sign one, believe me."

"Oh, Nick, I didn't mean you. I'm sorry. I just meant in general."

"Wouldn't it be better if they wore it and felt really bad because they'd dumped you?" I asked.

"No," Jazzi said.

"Let's change the subject," Dad said. "Who wants this ice cream?"

I had plans for my Jazzi-free weekend. The first thing Dad and I did was go to the pool and he held the hoop for me to dive through. We had pies for lunch, which we never had when Jazzi was around. And in the afternoon we played games. I beat him four out of nine games of advanced connectors. He played randomly, whereas I had real strategy.

We were to go to Bella Mama's for pizza and then to the movies but the phone rang.

"If that's Jazzi," I hissed at him, but he silenced me with a warning look.

"Hello? No, of course not, darling. What's wrong?"

It *was* Jazzi. I didn't want to hear anything more, but I didn't want to let him talk to her in private either, so I poured myself a glass of juice and sat down at the kitchen table. Served him right for not having a cordless phone like everyone else.

"Darling, that's terrible. No . . . well, I don't know. You've got notice, at least. Maybe the son will want to keep tenants . . . Oh, that complicates things, doesn't it? Still, I'm sure we can find you somewhere . . . Of course I'll help. More than happy, darling, after all the things you do for me. No, it won't be any trouble . . . Don't you worry about anything, darling. Maybe you'd like . . . Just a minute, I'll check something . . ."

I knew what was coming. I wanted to put my fingers in my ears but I couldn't because Dad had his best puppy-dog look on.

"Bee, sweetheart, Jazzi's upset. The old lady who owned her flat has died, and the son's given her notice. I know we've organized this weekend together, but she is terribly upset. Would it be okay with you if she joined us for dinner and the movies? Please?"

Somehow Dad made his brown eyes all soft and then he ducked his head the way he does when he really wants something, like the last piece of chocolate. I can't say no when he looks like that.

"You'll just talk about the flat and everything."

"Not until you go to bed, I promise."

"I'm staying up late tonight, remember."

"We still won't talk about it. Well, at least not after Jazzi's told us the whole story, okay?"

"The whole story will take *hours*. It will be boring."

"She's upset, sweetie. If one of your friends was upset, you'd want to help."

"Not if it was going to be boring and take forever."

"Bee, please?"

"Tell her she can only talk about the flat for five minutes, okay?"

"It's a deal."

I timed her and she talked for fifteen minutes and thirty seconds exactly before the pizza arrived. But she did apologize for interrupting my weekend with Dad and she looked pretty terrible, as though she hadn't slept much, so I sort of forgave her. Also I had pizza and tiramisu which is just the best thing you can eat, and I had a choc top at the movies, too, and neither Jazzi nor Dad said anything, although ordinarily the rule is that you can have dessert and no choc top or a choc top and no dessert.

But the next morning, of course, she was there and Dad wouldn't do anything with me, as he was too busy looking up flats for rent online. We didn't even have the breakfast I wanted—pancakes and maple syrup.

There were no eggs and Dad wouldn't go to the supermarket because Jazzi wanted to start looking that very morning, and "No, Bee, it couldn't wait." I had toast with the last of the jam, the awful last bits that everyone else leaves because there are bits of butter in them and even an ant or two. Dad claimed that the ants were toast crumbs and washed them quickly down the sink before I had a chance to point out the little legs to him.

It was shortly after that that Jazzi burst into tears. I'd never seen her cry before, not really cry out loud. It was interesting. Her mascara smudged all over her face and she bit her lipstick off so her lips went totally pale. She put her hands over her face as though she didn't want us to see her, but all that did was mess up her hair.

"Everything is so expensive," she said. "I can't believe it. I'll never find anywhere."

"Maybe you have to move to a slightly different area," Dad said, patting her awkwardly. "I'm sure we can find somewhere, Jazzi."

"I was so happy there," she sobbed. "I was just so happy."

It sounded to me as though she didn't think she could ever be happy again. I'd only been to her flat a few times. It wasn't *child-friendly* so Jazzi tended to come to our place unless I stayed with Nanna or Uncle Rob and Aunty Maree. It didn't look unfriendly to me, but it was pretty small and there were a lot of things in it. It wasn't a place you could stretch out in. Even the kitchen was tiny. If you had dinner there, you had to clear the table in Jazzi's study or else sit on the floor in the lounge room and eat from the coffee table, which I quite enjoyed doing. It was very Japanese. We'd learned about that at school. Dad said it gave him a cramp, though.

"Maybe you can get somewhere bigger," I said, trying to be helpful and positive. "You know, a proper place with a kitchen table. That would be good because then you could make stuff in the study and never have to clear it away."

Jazzi made weird things. She called them dolls but some of them didn't have any faces and some were kind of spooky. Others didn't have any clothes on and their rude bits were showing. She gave me one, not one of the rude ones, but one of the faceless ones. I didn't like it and I kept it up on a shelf in my cupboard so I didn't have to look at it.

"I'll never find anywhere bigger," Jazzi sniffed snottily, "not for the kind of money I can afford. I'll end up living in a cupboard somewhere—horrible."

I gave up then and stomped off to write a note to Fifi and Lulu. I knew it would take ages before Dad found it, but I didn't care. I had to complain to someone, so this is what I wrote:

Dear Lulu and Fifi,

All she's done is cry all morning, and all Dad's done is pat her and keep looking for places to rent on the Net. I wanted pancakes but no one would go to the supermarket for eggs. There were ants in the jam. I don't see why our weekend has to be ruined because some old lady has died and Jazzi has to find another flat. And who heard of a grown-up crying over something like that? My mother wouldn't have. She was a positive person. Dad always says you shouldn't be negative, but he didn't say that to Jazzi. Not once.

Love,

Bee

I left the letter in Lulu and Fifi's letter box. There wasn't anything to do, so I made a few fairy houses down near the tree ferns and wondered if the fairies ever used my houses. Once Sally had come over and we'd both made one. It was still there. Sally had put a little pebble fence around it and we'd even made a fairy birdbath from an old shell. It was the best fairy house. The ones I made by myself didn't look half as good. I stuck a cockatoo feather in the front of one, but it looked too big and I thought it might scare the fairies away, so I put the feather in my ponytail instead. That made me an Indian so I whooped around for a while and pretended to stalk some buffalo, but then Honey, the dog from next door, spotted me, so she stopped being a buffalo and I patted her tummy through the fence for a while. I thought about ringing Sally and seeing if she could come over and play, but then I remembered she wasn't talking to me.

It wasn't fair. No one was talking to me.

Inside the house, Dad and Jazzi were still hunched over the computer. Jazzi had the box of tissues on the arm of her chair. They were no longer looking at flats, though. There were all these figures on the screen and Dad was shaking his head at them in a sad kind of way.

"So much for my Jazzi-free weekend," I told him when he came to tuck me in that night.

"Bee," he said, sitting on the end of my bed, "I know you and Jazzi have had some differences but basically you'd say you both got along, wouldn't you? I know she's very fond of you."

I shrugged.

"Because I'm thinking of asking her if she'd like to move in with us." Dad spoke very quickly as if he didn't want to give me a chance to say anything at all. "She hasn't any family, you know, and we get along so well. She's really enriched my life, sweetheart. I love her very much. No one, and I mean that, Bee, no one could ever replace your mother, and I don't expect you to think of

Jazzi as your mother at all, and Jazzi wouldn't either. But I think we could all be very happy together."

I wanted to tell him that Jazzi did have family, that Harley was her brother, but I couldn't work out what to say, so instead I said, "Well, that's just great. Now I'll never have any Jazzi-free time. It will always be you, her, and me. What was wrong with the way it was?"

"I was lonely," Dad said, "and when I saw her that night at Trivia, I knew she was the most interesting woman in the room, but I thought she was bound to have a boyfriend. I was right about the first thing, but, fortunately for me, I was wrong about the second. I really want us all to live together, Bee. She's smart, she's pretty, she's creative, and she makes me laugh. We need each other."

"What about me?"

"Sweetheart, you're my best girl. You always will be. But you'll get older, and you'll move out and leave your poor old dad. You'll fall in love and marry someone and then where will I be?"

"You could be like Stan. He's happy."

"Only because he lives next door to your nanna!"

"Why can't you and Jazzi live next door to each other then?"

"Come on, Bee, look on the positive side. You'll have someone to take you clothes shopping, someone to teach you how to cook, and someone to do all those girlie things with. You need someone like that."

"I don't care," I said. "I don't care if she moves in or if she doesn't. I couldn't care less. I'm too tired."

I rolled over and pretended to go to sleep. Dad stayed on the end of my bed for ages but he didn't say anything else and neither did I.

Moving in

I didn't want to tell Sally and Lucy at school that Jazzi was going to be my stepmother, but Jazzi told them herself.

"Well, here we are," she said when she picked me up. "Hello, Sally, hello, Lucy. Has Beatrice told you the news?"

"No," Sally said, "*Beatrice* hasn't."

"I'm moving in with Nick, Beatrice's father, so the first thing we must do is to celebrate that by you girls coming over for a play as soon as I've settled in."

"Told you so," Lucy hissed behind Jazzi's back.

"We'll make cupcakes," Jazzi continued, "with pink icing."

"That would be lovely," Sally said politely.

"And you must call me Jazzi, just like Beatrice does. Now, if you could just introduce me to your mothers, I can get your phone numbers."

She acted just like a real mother and I didn't like it, but there was nothing I could do about it. She wrote their phone numbers down in her little pocket diary and discussed playdates with the other mothers.

The next day at school Sally said, "So she *is* your stepmother now."

"She's pretty cool," Lucy said. "Cupcakes sound good. Does she always make yummy things?"

"Always," I said, keeping my fingers crossed behind my back. "She makes scones practically every afternoon after school, and we eat them with strawberry jam and cream. She's going to be a great stepmum."

"Every afternoon?" Lucy sounded wistful.

"Nearly," I said. "On Fridays she makes chocolate ice cream with big lumps of real chocolate in it."

"She does not," Sally said sharply. "No one makes ice cream; you have to buy it."

"Jazzi makes it," I said. "And sometimes it's even got marshmallows in it and hundreds and thousands sprinkled on top."

Lucy and Sally looked at each other.

"I think you're lying, Bee," Sally said, "because you don't make ice cream, you buy it, and anyway you told me once ages ago that she didn't let you have anything unhealthy."

"That was before," I said. "This is now."

"You're still lying."

"Am not."

"Her fingers are crossed," Lucy said.

"No, they aren't." I waved my fingers in their faces. "See!"

"They were, though, I saw them."

"You two are impossible," I said and walked off to play Pick Up Papers. I was beginning to like Pick Up Papers.

At home, all that Dad and Jazzi talked about was The Big Day. Dad had decided to paint the lounge room just for Jazzi moving in, so we all looked at paint strips. I wanted Mountain Mist, but they decided on Natural Linen.

"What's the point of even painting it, if it's just going to be the same color?" I asked, but they were too busy measuring a space to see if the fold-down desk Jazzi's mother had left her would fit between Dad's big bookcase and the fish tank.

"I'd like my bedroom painted," I said. "I could have Mountain Mist in my room. I'd like a purple room, particularly if I could have a new quilt. I've had that Teddy Bear one ever since I can remember."

"I think my little quilt could go up on that wall. The colors would tone in nicely, don't you think, Nick?"

"I think you know much more about that kind of thing than I do," Dad said, putting his arm around her, "and I'm counting on you getting our house shipshape again."

"So painting my room would be a good thing," I said, "in terms of the shipshapedness of everything."

But they didn't hear me, or they weren't listening.

I cut the Mountain Mist square out from the paint strip and put it on the fridge with a note, *For Bee's room!* and wrote to the guinea pigs on the rest of the strip.

Dear Fifi and Lulu,
It is all mad in the big house. You are lucky to be here in your own little cubby with no one moving in. In fact, you are lucky to be guinea pigs. If no one paints my room Mountain Mist, which is the color I would really like it to be, can I come and live with both of you, please? I promise not to fuss or want to put anything big in too small a space.
Love,
The girl who feeds you, Bee-the-best

The next morning I got a note back:

Dear Bee-the-best-girl,
We both think Mountain Mist sounds like a very romantic color. Would you get sick of living in a romantic room, though? You could come and live with

us, but Fifi has the left-hand side of our hutch and Lulu has the right, so you'd have to squeeze up between us. We'd all be very warm at night.

Love,

Fifi and Lulu, the eaters

"I wouldn't get sick of Mountain Mist," I told Dad as he drove me to school. "Honest I wouldn't, Dad. It's the color I really want my room."

"Bee, let me just get the lounge room painted first, okay? Then we can discuss your room. First things first. Jazzi has to move in, and then we can assess what other changes need to be made."

Jazzi didn't seem to have a first things first problem.

"I'd like to have a dinner party, Nick darling," she said, "to celebrate my move. Our move."

"Of course, darling. I think that's a great idea. But let's move first, shall we?"

"I'd like Sam and Rowena to come, since they were responsible for us meeting, and Ro's been my best friend for ages, and I'd like your, you know, Lindy's brother and his wife—it sounds strange to say that. But I'd like us all to get along and I know how important they are in your life and we should meet. It's strange that we haven't, really. Patricia, of course, she'll have to come."

"Sure. But, sweetheart, I think we need to get you moved before we start planning dinner parties."

"Will I be there?"

"Of course, Beatrice. You can help me with the preparations. You could . . . let me see . . . help choose the flowers."

"So it won't be a barbecue?"

"I suppose we could have something on the back deck. Although there might be mosquitoes. Also, I think Patricia might prefer to be indoors."

"If you're going to invite Nanna, you'd better ask Stan as well."

"Of course," Jazzi said.

"And what about Harley?" I said. "You'll have to invite Harley."

"Who is Harley?" asked Dad.

I stared at Jazzi wildly, trying to say sorry without actually saying anything, but she wouldn't look at me.

"So," Dad said, looking from me to Jazzi, "who is Harley?"

"Harley is my brother," Jazzi whispered.

"I'm sorry," I said almost at the same time. "I didn't mean to tell. It just slipped out."

"Didn't mean to tell what, Bee?"

Dad's voice was his dangerously quiet one. It meant, "Have a bath or else. Go to bed without arguing now. No, you cannot have any more ice cream, *don't ask again*."

"Nothing," I said.

"Jazzi, can you explain this?"

"Harley is my brother," Jazzi whispered again. "He's not . . . well. I didn't tell you. I didn't want you to think . . . I should have said something. I'm sorry."

"He's really nice, Dad. Harley is really nice. You wouldn't know there was anything wrong with him, really."

"What exactly is wrong with Harley, and why has Bee met this secret person but I haven't yet had the pleasure?"

"He's not secret," Jazzi said. "I just don't like to talk about him. But he's not secret. If you'd asked me, I would have told you."

"I'm sure I did ask if you had any brothers or sisters. I can remember asking, actually. I asked you in front of Rowena and Sam, the first night I met you."

"You asked Rowena, and she said no. I didn't say anything."

"So your best friend doesn't know you have a brother?"

"Not really."

"Not really?"

"I think we should discuss this in private, Nick."

They discussed it privately for a very long time. I watched three TV programs downstairs while they talked, and we got home-delivered pizza and I was allowed to eat it in front of the TV which was very strange. They discussed it right up to my bedtime,

75

when Dad stopped discussing long enough to tuck me in, but they were still deep in conversation when I wandered out hours later to get a drink of water.

The result of all the talk was that Harley was invited to the dinner party, too. I was kind of pleased about that. I didn't think Harley should miss out. I thought about his tea bags and his sticky buns and I knew Harley would like to come to dinner.

Jazzi moved in on a Friday and by the following Monday her stuff had found its way into all of our cupboards and onto all of our shelves. Her pictures hung next to our tree fern and creek photos. In Dad's bedroom, her clothes hung next to his in the wardrobe. I crept down and looked. He'd crammed all his work clothes up at one end while Jazzi's skirts and dresses rustled roomily at the other.

Only my room was a Jazzi-free zone, if you didn't count that doll, sitting with her face to the wall in my cupboard. I wrote to Fifi and Lulu:

Dear Fifi and Lulu,

It's really scary, her stuff is everywhere. It's not that I don't like her stuff. She has much nicer mugs than we have. None of hers are chipped. She's got a plate I like, too, with chooks on it. They have bright red tails and yellow beaks. She said I could use it

anytime. But our lives have totally changed and Dad doesn't seem to know that. He just keeps looking at her with this dopey grin while she makes them both tea in her teapot. Dad used to have tea bags. Now we have tea in a pot and she'll teach me to make it. What's wrong with tea bags anyway? I don't get it.
Love,
Bee (who feels mopey)

They wrote back:

Dear mopey Bee,
In Japan they have a beautiful tea ceremony and they use cups that are so thin you can see the shadow of your fingers through them. Perhaps J. just enjoys pouring tea from a pot? All change is scary. Like when you bought us from the pet shop we thought anything could happen. Who is this girl? we thought. Will she eat us? we wondered. "Will we be happy?" we asked each other. But we are and you might be, too. The chook plate sounds rather nice. Are chooks anything like us? Have you ever seen a guinea pig plate?
Love,
Fifi and Lulu (who would like some more celery, please)

The Toasterpede

Almost as soon as she'd moved in, Jazzi started cleaning. She picked me up from school on Wednesday and we went straight to the supermarket, but not to buy food. Jazzi piled her cart high with cleaning products. There was carpet spotter, floor polish, counter cleaner, glass cleaner, and mold buster.

"We don't need all this," I told her. "Honest, Jazzi, I wouldn't waste your money. Dad and I have never cleaned that much."

"I know," she answered, rather grimly I thought, as she added furniture polish, "but we will, Beatrice. You and I will clean that poor house until it shines."

She actually looked pleased about it, as though she'd announced a holiday at the beach instead of a cleaning frenzy.

"I don't think I can help," I said. "I think I might be allergic to all this . . . stuff. I think I come out in spots. That's probably why we don't do so much cleaning. So, Jazzi, I think we should just put it all back and buy some ice cream instead."

Jazzi just snorted.

"I just don't see the point," I said later, when we'd lifted every last thing off the kitchen counter and she was spraying it viciously. "It's not as if our food touches this. Why can't we just wipe around the things?"

"Beatrice, I know your breakfast toast was in direct contact with this counter this morning."

"Only for a minute, just until I remembered the plate. Shall I clean out the toaster then?"

"Over the sink, please, and pull the crumb tray out. I'm sure that hasn't been done for years."

A mountain of crumbs fell into the sink. And Jazzi was right, it had been a long time. There were a couple of raisins in it and we only had raisin toast in winter. I gave the toaster a little tap, just to make sure there weren't more raisins sticking to the bottom and out fell something wriggly.

I screamed and nearly dropped the toaster. "It's alive!"

"My heavens," Jazzi said, peering at the thing, "it

looks like a very hairy centipede. Quick, Beatrice, pop a glass over it. Don't let it go down the plughole."

"You're mad. I'm not touching it."

Jazzi slammed a glass over The Thing and we both watched it move all its hairy legs wildly as it scurried around, trying to get out. Then Jazzi got a piece of cardboard and slipped it quickly between The Hairy-legged Thing and the sink, flipped it up, knocked the cardboard, and The Thing was trapped in the bottom of the glass.

"What are you going to do with it?" I backed away. How could Jazzi trap this thing, but not want to hold Lulu or Fifi? She was plain weird.

"I want to show your dad." Jazzi grinned at me and she looked younger. "This could be the last of the Toasterpedes, Beatrice. It may even be a new discovery. How many people do you know who have a Toasterpede? Let's put him—or her—somewhere very safe. We don't want to knock him over."

I had hoped that the Toasterpede would put Jazzi off her cleaning. After all, if that could live in our toaster, which was used every day, what could be at the bottom of the pantry? But nothing put Jazzi off.

I had to do the cupboard doors while Jazzi scrubbed the microwave.

"The problem with doing this," I said, "is that if I don't do all of them, the clean ones are going to look too clean."

"So you'll do all of them." Jazzi had abandoned the scourer and was attacking the inside of the microwave with a small plastic picnic knife.

"I suppose that could be the answer," I told her bottom which waggled from side to side as she jabbed around with the knife, "but I think my elbow is starting to ache."

"Just keep going, Beatrice."

There were stains that it almost hurt to remove, because they were part of my life. Like the bit of my last birthday cake when Dad dropped the chocolate he'd burned in the microwave. I thought about mentioning to Jazzi that we weren't just cleaning cupboards but cleaning out my memories, but her bottom looked too fierce.

When I'd done the cupboards, we stacked the chairs on the kitchen table and Jazzi swept up, with me following with the dustpan and brush.

"I think we're doing this too soon. After all, Jazzi, you haven't even cooked for the dinner party, so there'll be more dropped things on the floor after that. Wouldn't it be better to do the floors *after* the dinner party?"

"I don't drop things when I cook." Jazzi turned around so suddenly that the dustpan fell out of my hands. She pressed her lips together until they went white.

"Sorry," I said. "It's just that you startled me. Sorry. I'll clean it up."

"Yes, you will."

Jazzi had tucked her hair up in a purple bandana that went with her checked trousers. The back of her neck was all sweaty. She scrubbed the floor with a scrubbing brush, starting at the kitchen sink and working her way back, past the table and chairs and right to the hallway carpet. Some of the dark streaks on our lino tiles turned out to be dirt, but some were definitely part of the swirly pattern.

She was going to do the fridge, but when we pulled out some old pineapple in an ancient tin, Jazzi shook her head.

"We should recycle," she said, "but this is a biochemical hazard." And she marched it straight to the outside bin with some old jars of dubious jam.

"I'm tired," she announced when she came back in. "I think we deserve a break, Beatrice. See if you can find anything nice in the freezer."

There were four chocolate ice-cream bars in the freezer. We ate two and watched TV while we waited for Dad to come home and admire our work.

He thought the Toasterpede might be one of a kind, but we let it out into the front garden just in case there was another one lurking around.

"Won't it be a bit cold for it?" I asked. "After all, it's used to living in the toaster."

"I think if it can survive that, it must be pretty tough," he said.

"It's a clear night," Jazzi said, linking her arm through Dad's and looking up. "Look, Beatrice, can you see the Southern Cross?"

"And the Saucepan," I said, "the Big Dipper."

"Oh, that reminds me, Nick. Can I get rid of a couple of your saucepans? We simply don't have room for them all, and mine are copper-bottomed, much better for conducting heat."

"Anything you want, Jazzi."

"Thank you, darling."

I thought they were going to kiss then, so I yawned loudly and went inside.

Jazzi didn't only clean for the big dinner. She spread cookbooks across the kitchen table and discussed different meals endlessly.

"Can't we just get pizza?" I was sick of hearing about food I'd never heard of before.

"You can't go wrong with a roast," Dad said helpfully. "Everyone loves a roast."

"Harley doesn't. He won't eat anything that bleeds."

"Pizza doesn't bleed," I said, "and you can get pineapple on the vegetarian if you ask."

"I can't decide between Italian—Harley could have cannelloni then, or something more Eastern fusion—a kind of soba noodle salad with ginger sauce and maybe some sushi."

"Italian sounds more . . . filling," Dad said.

"Pizza's Italian," I said. "Couldn't we have pizza? I miss pizza."

"Bee, put pizza right out of your head, okay? There will be no pizza on Saturday night."

The good thing about Jazzi living with us was that she called me Bee more than she used to.

I helped her set the table on Saturday afternoon. She found a silver candelabra at the back of one of our cupboards and put it in the center of the crisp white tablecloth. She'd bought flowers—expensive daisies that had to be wired by the florist so their pale pink heads didn't droop.

Each place was set with one of Jazzi's old plates, and she used her cutlery, which matched and was smarter than ours, although stranger too, with odd big-bladed knives, and forks that had only three prongs. Her champagne flutes were dark red with spiraling stems.

"It's so beautiful," I said after we'd folded her thick napkins into crowns and put them at everyone's place. "It's just beautiful."

She smiled at me and put her arm around my shoulders. "We've done well," she said.

"Magnificent," Dad said, coming up behind us and putting his arms around both of us. "I can't remember the last time this table was extended. It must have been years ago, when your mother was alive, Bee, probably Christmastime. Lindy loved Christmas."

I wondered if Jazzi minded Dad mentioning Mum like that. It would be hard loving someone who had loved someone else before you. You'd know all the time that they'd loved the other person and missed them. You might feel second-best. Kind of the way I feel when Lucy plays with me and I know it's only because Sally's away sick.

"It's Jazzi's dinner," I said to him when I could get him alone for a minute. "I don't think you should talk about Mum."

"I didn't talk about her, Bee."

"You did, Dad, you mentioned her. I don't think you should tonight."

"I'm sure Jazzi didn't mind, Bee. I doubt that she even noticed. I hardly noticed myself."

But Jazzi had noticed. I was certain of that. Sometimes Dad just didn't pay quite enough attention.

The dinner

Just before seven o'clock, Jazzi lit the candles. She wore a silky top with flowers on it almost the exact pink of the daisies, and she'd brushed her hair up to a knot on the top of her head, combed her eyebrows, and put on dark red glittery earrings. She'd persuaded Dad to change out of his weekend work-around-the-house clothes into a soft, dark blue shirt I'd never seen before. I felt drab beside them, still in my jeans and a T-shirt that was almost too small for me.

"Come on, Bee," Jazzi said, looking me up and down. "Do you want me to do your hair?"

"Well, okay, if you don't pull it." Dad always pulled

at it when he tried to brush out the knots and it hurt worse than almost anything.

"I won't. I'll do it in little bunches and we'll have a look through your wardrobe. I think I've seen a lovely skirt in there which would be just the thing for dinner."

I didn't have time to wonder how she'd seen skirts in my wardrobe, because within seconds it seemed she'd brushed my hair, holding it at the roots the way you have to, and wound it into little balls above my ears. Then she'd found the skirt, one that Nanna had bought me that I'd forgotten about because it was for going out, and, without my having to ask her, turned her back while I slipped it on.

"Hold on one moment, Bee, you just need something over that T-shirt. Wait here." And Jazzi vanished, leaving me to look at my hair in the mirror. It looked good. She'd just wound it around so that it looked like little shells. I was worried that it might fall out and shook my head fiercely a couple of times but the shells stayed put.

"Here," Jazzi said, "I think this is just the extra touch your outfit needs, and then I've got this for your hair."

She threw a lacy poncho over my head. It was decorated with blue and pink velvet flowers at the front. I touched them and they were just as soft as they looked. The flower that went into one of my hair-shells was the same blue.

"Beautiful," Jazzi said, "just beautiful. Look at that, Bee. You are gorgeous. And the blue matches your dad's shirt. I just love it when things work like that, don't you?"

I'd never thought of clothes working before. They either fit or they didn't. Or you liked them or you didn't—although often I wasn't really sure if I liked something until someone else did. Or it would turn out that I liked something wrong—like the dress with the sash that I begged Nanna to buy and Sally laughed at so I couldn't ever wear it.

But when I went back out to the table all set up in the dining nook, the wired daisies with their big faces, the glasses glittering in the candlelight, and Dad opening a bottle of wine to breathe while Jazzi put a basket of bread on the table, I thought I knew what she meant. For just those moments we could have been a family in a film.

Then the new doorbell pealed out and our guests arrived.

Nanna and Stan were first, of course. Stan had combed his mustache so it draped neatly around his mouth. Nanna had lipstick on, and I hoped she'd only kiss me lightly so I wouldn't have to scrub it off.

"Doesn't your hair look lovely, Bee, and what a pretty poncho. Jazzi, that pink suits you. How are you, my dear? Nick, you're looking relaxed!" Nanna bustled through. "I wasn't sure what to bring, Jazzi, so in the end I just brought this. A silly hostess gift, I know, quite ridiculous really, but there you are. I thought you might like it."

"Oh, my god, Patricia. A knitting magazine. How wonderful."

"It's the latest from America," Nanna said. "Sorry, Nick dear, but Stan brought wine, of course."

"I did. Good wine, Nick. Good wine to go with the good food this delightful girl will have cooked for us."

The doorbell went again and this time I opened it as Jazzi and Nanna were still flipping through the pages oohing and aahing and Dad and Stan were talking about wine.

"Hello, darling Beatrice." Rowena, Jazzi's best friend, was standing at the door.

"It's Bee," I said. If Jazzi was going to be living here, her best friend had better know the right thing to call me.

"Oh, I'm sorry. Jazzi always says Beatrice."

"It's okay, I'm retraining her," I whispered. I liked Rowena. She had short, spiky hair and wore smudged dark eyeliner, so she looked like an exotic panda. She was a textile artist and sold her stuff, and sometimes Jazzi's dolls, at markets. Sam loomed behind her.

"Bee," he said. "Yes, I thought it was. That's what your dad always calls you."

Sam was a teacher. They're trained to listen for that kind of thing, so I wasn't surprised.

Then Uncle Rob arrived with Aunty Maree and everyone crowded into the dining nook exclaiming over the flowers and what everyone else was wearing and Dad and Stan poured wine and I had lemonade.

"Well," Uncle Rob said when we all had our glasses filled, "I think we should have a toast: To Nick and Jazzi—health, happiness, and love."

"We can't toast yet," I said. "Harley's not here."

"Who's Harley?"

"My brother," Jazzi said, not looking at anyone.

"I didn't know you had a brother, Jazzi," Rowena said, and I could tell she was upset.

"We don't see each other very often," Jazzi said. "You'll know why. If he shows up."

Just as she said that, the front door pealed again.

"I'll get it," Jazzi said quickly. "You all sit down at the table."

"I had no idea," Rowena said, looking around us all. "I thought she was an only child. I've known Jazzi for nearly seven years, and I didn't know she had a brother."

"Ssh," Sam said, "it's okay."

"Everyone," Jazzi said, "this is Harley. Harley . . ."

"This is Everyone. Hello, Everyone. I hope I'm not late. I'll sit here, thanks Jasmine, I like to be able to see out." He pulled out the seat next to me, sat down, and then almost immediately got up again. "Did Everyone see my T-shirt?"

His T-shirt was black and had the word *Neurotic* written right across it in old-fashioned curly writing.

"Yes," Uncle Rob said, "they're a band of some sort, aren't they?"

"It's a mental condition," Harley corrected him. "I just want you to know that I don't have it. It's not what I have. In case anyone was wondering."

"That's good to know," Sam said, "but I think most people are a bit neurotic, aren't they?"

"I might have OCD. That is a neurotic disorder, but it's not commonly thought of as being neurotic. The T-shirt isn't a label. I just liked the look of it."

"We didn't think it was a label," Jazzi said. "No one thought that." Her voice was very soft, as though she was talking to a child. "Can I get you a glass of lemonade?"

"I'll have what you're having," Harley said, pointing to her glass. "That looks nice."

"It won't go with your tablets," Jazzi said. "Lemonade would be nicer."

"You're always trying to keep the best things for yourself," Harley said. "I want some of what you've got."

I waited for Jazzi to give him a lecture, but she just smiled a tight smile and poured a little wine into one of the red glasses.

"We're having a toast," she said to him, "to Nick and me."

"Toast with what? Jam? I hope it's not strawberry. I can't eat strawberries. Or raspberries. I don't eat red, Jazzi. Pink's okay if it's on the top but not if it's inside."

"She didn't mean toast," I said, putting my hand over Harley's hand which was busy drawing the flower pattern of the tablecloth over and over again. He jumped when I touched him, but his hand stayed still under mine. "We're not having toast. It's a toast, when you congratulate people on something they've done. Then we'll have dinner and there's vegetarian for you. Jazzi made it specially."

"Specially for me?"

I nodded.

"So, no red?"

"No, it's orange. It's roast pumpkin and sweet potato cannelloni."

"Orange is good." Harley nodded. "I like orange, even when it's inside. So now we congratulate?"

"Yes," Uncle Rob said quickly, "now is a good time to congratulate Jazzi and Nick on their good fortune in finding each other. To Jazzi and Nick!"

Everyone raised their glasses and murmured, "To Jazzi and Nick."

"Nick the worrier," Harley said. "I can see which one he is. Hello, Nick the someone, not the everyone."

I was scared that Dad would be confused and say the wrong thing, but he was paying attention for once.

"Hello, Harley, I am pleased to meet you," he said and smiled one of his best smiles that went right from his eyes down practically to his chin.

"It isn't often I meet Jasmine's friends," Harley said. "We should have toasts to that, too."

"To meeting friends," Dad said, raising his glass again.

"Oh yes," Stan said, "and another toast, to Patreeeecia and me. Patreeeecia has consented to come with me on a . . . what do you call it?"

"A holiday, Stan," Nanna said. "That's what we're calling it."

"No, no. There is a better word. It is on the tip of my tongue. Yes—a road trip. We are going on a road trip of nostalgia, back to Lake Jindabyne and Eucumbene where I worked when I was a young man new to this country."

"A road trip?" Dad looked at Nanna.

"A holiday," Nanna said firmly. "Stan and I are going on a holiday."

"Together?"

"A romantic road trip." Stan beamed at us all. "Romantic and nostalgic."

"To Stan and Patreeeecia!" Harley said, sounding out Nanna's name the same way Stan had.

"You don't need to say it like that," I told him quietly, after we'd all had more sips. I didn't want Stan thinking Harley was having a go at him. "It's just Patricia really."

"I like Patreeecia," Harley said.

Really, I couldn't see why Jazzi had made such a fuss over Harley coming. Apart from the Patreeecia-thing, and rearranging everything on the table to show Uncle Rob and Dad just how he'd walked from his house to our place—not far at all and I thought it was pretty neat the way the saltshaker became the postbox at the corner and the salad bowl became the playground— and apart from calling Jazzi's beautiful profiterole tower '*profit rolls*' and refusing to eat them because they were part of the conspiracy, Harley seemed fine.

I suppose Jazzi was put out when he lay down on the couch without taking his shoes off, but he did explain that his feet smelled. I know she felt it wasn't particularly polite the way he went to sleep and, yes, he did snore very loudly, but she said herself it was the tablets he had to take. We couldn't wake him up, so he stayed there all night. Jazzi threw a blanket over him and tucked a pillow under his head.

"I'm sorry about this, Nick," she kept saying, but Dad didn't mind and everyone else just stayed sitting around the table talking. After all, people go to sleep on couches all the time. What else is a couch for?

In the morning we all walked Harley home, and Jazzi seemed happier somehow. She smiled more and even laughed at a long, not very funny joke Harley told. She held Dad's hand and every so often I'd see them look at each other and it made me feel as though I'd overheard a secret whispered by someone—a nice secret, though, not a nasty one.

Harley's butterflies

I wanted to be happy because Dad was happy and Nanna told me to be happy and even I could see that Jazzi had brought some good things into our life. There was the bread she made almost every day so we had fresh stuff, whereas before I always had to check for mold, because Dad forgot sometimes. There was my scarf which Jazzi fixed for me by making some big wool flowers which we sewed to the narrow end bit. They were a design feature. Sally and Lucy liked it so much they had asked me to make them one each.

They liked the way she did my hair too, and they thought my new runners with the glittery laces were pretty cool. Jazzi was good at organizing things and sometimes they came over after school to play.

But there were bad things, too. She made me go to bed strictly at bedtime. She made me do my homework every afternoon, and if I didn't have any I had to read aloud to her for at least twenty minutes. I had to make my bed every morning and clean my room up once a week. She even made me vacuum under the bed. She was utterly ruthless when it came to food. I had to eat fish, chops, peas and beans, sweet potato, and brown rice. It wasn't any use telling her I couldn't cut chops up. She just sat there and told me to keep trying.

I think it was the skirt she made for me which started the problem. Even that was a good-Jazzi thing. She let me choose the material and then she showed me how to cut it out on a big cardboard cutting board she unfolded on the lounge-room floor.

The problem was that when Dad got home he stepped on one of the pins that must have fallen out of the pin box when I accidentally kicked it over. It went in quite deeply and he said some things he shouldn't have. When we'd all calmed down, he suggested that Jazzi use the spare room for her sewing room.

"Clear out anything in it," he said. "It's only old stuff that no one wants anymore. I think that will be the best thing. We can move that little table in, the one that's cluttering up the kitchen, and you'll have somewhere to do this kind of stuff without having to worry about clearing it up until you've actually finished. I think this will bruise. It went in quite deeply."

"Nick, I'm so sorry. I thought we'd got all the pins up."

"Never mind, these things happen." Dad limped across the floor. "It won't require amputation!"

I had an uneasy feeling about the spare room and halfway through PE it came to me. My box was in the bottom of the built-in wardrobe. But Jazzi wouldn't throw it out, would she? She'd know it was mine, with my things in it, and she'd put it in my room. Jazzi would have to do that; she kept all sorts of old things herself.

I didn't get a chance to ask Jazzi about the box because it was a Harley day, only more special because Harley wanted to visit his and Jazzi's mother, so we drove to Springvale Cemetery. Harley had brought a mug to put at the grave. He said it would last longer than Jazzi's flowers and it was just as pretty. Jazzi said it would get stolen. Harley said people didn't rob graves. Jazzi said they did.

"I'm afraid they do, Harley," I said. "They did in Egypt, remember? They robbed the pyramids. I saw the movie."

"They died," Harley said. "They died from a curse. That's it, then. I'll curse Mum's mug and no one will steal it."

"That's ridiculous, Harley, you can't curse it. Don't be silly."

"Of course I can curse it. Watch me." He screwed up his face and put his hands in his hair, the way Jazzi did when she read the morning paper. We waited.

"Your mother is buried here, too, isn't she, Bee? Do you want to . . . ?"

"Maybe next time. I don't think she's buried, actually, I think she was cremated and then Dad took some of the ashes down to Apollo Bay, where they'd spent their honeymoon."

"There's probably a plaque here though," Jazzi said, looking around her. "We could put some flowers there, if you like, next time."

"Ssh," Harley said, "I'm trying to get the last word!"

I thought about my mother, how maybe she'd feel odd that Harley and Jazzi's mother was getting a mug with roses on it and a bunch of yellow flowers and she wasn't getting anything. Would she mind? Or would she understand that I didn't know all this was going to happen and was unprepared? Would she love me anyway? Jazzi fiddled with the yellow flowers and Harley sat down on the ground, his eyes squeezed shut in concentration.

"Got it!" he said, stumbling to his feet. He put the mug down on the headstone and waved his arms in the air above his mother's grave so that it looked as though he was trying to shoo away flies or mosquitoes.

"Fiend, rogue, robber, thief,

linger not by my mother's grave

or the curse of the devil's teeth

will smite you down and nothing save."

"That was good," I said. "Did you just think of it then?"

"He was always good at English," Jazzi said. "That and art were his best subjects."

"They still are," Harley said. "Did I tell you I'm going to be in an exhibition? You'll have to come. We're all loonies but it will be good. Powerful, that's what Tony said, a powerful statement about loonies." He threw back his head and laughed. It was a strange sound to hear in a cemetery and both Jazzi and I looked around, but there didn't seem to be anyone close to us.

"You don't think that's too much pressure, do you, Harley? Have you done the work yet? Do you feel okay about it?"

"I don't like Arthur. He's another one. His work is too dark, too much black. It won't show up well, I keep telling Tony. It's too dark. You can't see what it's about. But Tony said it was strong work. Muscular, he called it. Flabby, I call it. What's muscular about just using black black black? There's no way back. I said, 'Arthur, stop mucking around in the murk and reach for some stars, man. Show us some glimmers, simmer some cerise, glow some yellow, gild the darkness with a bit of gilt.' He flicked paint on my best shirt, Jasmine. You'll have to wash it for me before the exhibition. You will, won't you? Please?"

"Of course I will, Harley. When does it open? Do we get invitations?"

"Yes, yes. Tony's doing all that. He's a bureaucratic bureaucrat. But he's not black. He glimmers with a bit of gold heart now and then. He's all right. Do you want to put your flowers in my cursed mug?"

"No," Jazzi said, "they don't need water. They're everlasting daisies and they won't fit without me cutting the stems."

"You're right, it's probably better this way. She gets two things rather than two-things-made-into-one-thing. Okay, can we go now, Jasmine? We've said hello to Mum and left some flowers, painted and real. Can we go now and eat sticky buns? I'm sick of being surrounded by dead people."

"Ssssh," Jazzi said. "You might offend someone, Harley."

"They're all dead," Harley said. "How can I offend them? They're not listening, Jasmine, whatever way you look at it."

"Not them, the visitors. You might offend a visitor. Come on, then, let's go."

When we got to Harley's we saw the paintings and drawings he was going to exhibit. We couldn't help but see them—they were all over the kitchen and the lounge room of the house.

"How are Bill and Laura coping with all this?" Jazzi asked, hands on her hips, surveying the mess.

"It's art," Harley said. "They do what everyone else does, they simply pretend it doesn't exist."

"That's not true," came a voice from one of the couches, and the lady with the jabbing finger poked her head out from her newspaper. "We know it's there. We just try not to sit on it."

"Can't you keep these somewhere?" Jazzi said. "You'll end up ruining them. It's not just people sitting on them, Harley. They could get food on them."

Harley shrugged. "I don't want to be precious about them, Jasmine. Art belongs to everyone and everything."

"Yes, but not the tomato sauce." Jazzi pointed to the corner of a strange-looking piece that had labels from old jam jars and cigarette packets stuck on it.

"Oh, well." Harley took it from her and started ripping it up.

"Harley!"

"Well, you're right. It's not fit for anything but mouse consumption now." He put the pile of torn-up pieces in one corner of the lounge room. "They can nest their babies in an original Harley Raddle."

"Oh, Harley." Jazzi looked at him and I thought for a minute she was going to cry but instead she laughed.

Harley gave us a tour of the artworks. Some of them joined Consumer Collage in the mouse corner as we went. They weren't the kind of pictures I was used to seeing. They were "abstracted representation," Harley said, like when you have dreams and everything isn't quite real but it's ordinary enough to be familiar. In Harley's drawings, flowers turned into heads, which sat on top of dark clouds. Birds became men, fingers stretched into insects, which crawled across a desert of television sets and old antennae. I didn't like them much.

"Surreal," Jazzi said, tipping her head to one side as she looked at them all. "Definitely Dali-esque, Harley. I like this series particularly."

"So do I." Those three were the ones I *did* like, a series of faces on huge butterfly wings. Each wing had about three or four faces drawn on it. You could have easily mistaken the faces for patterns at first, but when you looked more closely they became wrinkled, beady-eyed and wispy-bearded, or just a detailed eye was visible, the outline of flared nostrils, or a section of pouted lips.

"You can have them, Jazzi and To Be, when the exhibition is over. I'll get Tony to mark sold on them as soon as they are hung up. You'll have to get them framed, Jazzi. You can have two and To Be can have one, because she's smaller. Worrier Nick will have to share yours, Jazzi, because I can't do any more. I've moved away from such dependence on reality, such narrative."

"Harley, you can't just give them away like that. What if these are the three that would sell? Then you've missed a sale."

"I can do what I want," Harley said and yawned loudly. "After all, they are mine, Jasmine. Anyway, you gave me one of your little angel guardian dolls. I painted a face on it, did I tell you? I couldn't bear the blank."

"That's good, Harley, you were supposed to paint a face on it. That's how it becomes your guardian doll. Or whatever kind it is. Well, thank you very much, Harley. We really do appreciate it."

"Yes, thank you, Harley. I've never owned a proper painting or drawing before."

Of course, when we got home, Harley's paintings and the exhibition were the only thing that was talked about and we all examined the invitation which had one of Harley's butterfly drawings on it and Jazzi told Dad how he'd given us that series.

I forgot all about my box and its precious things, which may or may not have been at the bottom of the wardrobe in Jazzi's sewing room.

Running away

I didn't get to look for my box for days after visiting Jazzi and Harley's mum, because there was an afternoon trip to the movies with Sally and an afternoon at the pool with Lucy and then Jazzi decided to enroll me for tennis lessons and when I finally got to see the room it was Friday afternoon.

You would expect a sewing room to be a plain, useful room. Jazzi's sewing room was like something out of the Arabian Nights stories. She'd hung this lovely mirrored quilt on one wall, and a big piece of rainbow-colored material billowed from the roof.

There was a small white-painted chest of drawers with bright blue flower handles near Jazzi's table, and a white bookcase held a collection of books about quilts and knitting and artists. A tall lamp stood in one corner of the room and there was a wall shelf on which perched some of Jazzi's dolls. A rocking chair in the other corner was covered with cushions and a big knitted throw. It was quite beautiful and I would have sat down and looked at some of the books, but I was on a mission.

When I opened the wardrobe, I was nearly suffocated by a pile of fabric that fell out. I stuffed it quickly back. I opened the other side of the wardrobe. More fabric was hung on coat hangers, a hanging rainbow. But my box was nowhere to be seen.

I raised the issue with Jazzi. That's what we did in our house now. We didn't just talk about things. We raised issues.

"You know that box of my stuff," I said. Jazzi was stuffing a chicken. The stuffing was green with chopped parsley. I don't know why we bother to eat parsley, really. It just tastes green—and not even a nice green. A dull, stodgy kind of green.

"No. What box?"

"The box at the bottom of the wardrobe in your sewing room."

"There wasn't a box of your stuff, Beatrice. If there had been, I would have put it in your room."

"It's not there. It's not in the bottom of the wardrobe either. There was a box of stuff in the bottom of the wardrobe. I know, because I put it there ages ago."

"There wasn't a box of your stuff, Beatrice."

"Yes, there was, Jazzi, honestly. It was a little cardboard box of stuff."

"There was a carton, I remember. Is that what you mean?"

"It had my stuff in it." I was trying to stay patient, but it was hard.

"Well, the carton I found had some weird old things in it, some of which I threw out and some of which I gave away."

"You didn't!"

"I did, Beatrice, yes."

"But that was my stuff."

"Well, it wasn't particular stuff. It was just a bunch of rubbish. That's all."

"There was my old bee bowl I used when I was a baby."

"There may have been something like that."

"It had flowers on the side and a bee on the inside."

"I don't remember," Jazzi said.

"It was important," I said. "It was the bowl my mother used to feed me from. And there was a skirt she made. It was moss green and had a bee flying to a flower appliquéd on it."

"Oh yes, I remember that," Jazzi said. "I thought it

107

was very pretty. I left that at the thrift shop for some other little girl to wear."

"That was my skirt," I wailed. "My mother made that skirt for me."

"Well, I didn't know that," Jazzi said. "Your father said to clear out anything that was in the room, so that's what I did."

"There was a little pincushion, too."

"It was torn," Jazzi said. "I just . . ."

"I bought that for my mum. I bought it for her on the last Mother's Day we ever had."

"Oh, Bee, I didn't know that. No one told me."

"They were my precious things. There was a spoon with a daisy on top."

"The daisy was chipped."

"And a glass with painted flowers on it."

"I didn't think. The flowers looked, I don't know, kind of . . ."

"I painted those flowers. It went with the pincushion." I was crying properly now. I'd rescued those things from Dad's big cleanout. They weren't precious to anyone else, I knew that when Dad tried to throw them out, and they weren't things like photographs that you could display anywhere, but they were special all the same.

"Oh, Bee." Jazzi turned away from the chicken and tried to hug me without touching me with her stuffing fingers. I tensed all my muscles so she couldn't, and we stood there awkwardly until she gave up. When she pulled away we were both crying, but I pretended not to see her tears.

"I hate you," I told her. "I really do. You've ruined my life, Jasmine."

I wouldn't come out for dinner that night. Even the roast chicken smell wasn't enough to coax me out. I pulled out all my photos of my mother and me and I started a gallery on my wall. I snuck out later, when they were watching TV, and stole the photograph of Dad and Mum on their wedding day from where Dad kept it in the top drawer of the side dresser, and I took the big one of Mum and me as a baby, for good measure. He didn't deserve them.

I stuck them in my schoolbag. I couldn't live with Dad and Jazzi any longer. I wasn't sure where I was going to go but I certainly didn't want to live with her. If you saw the old things *she* kept! A set of old jars with Flour, Sugar, and Tea on them, some little spoons—too little to even eat ice cream with—that had windmills on top, an old teapot with a cracked lid, and some hats no one would dream of wearing that Dad had to hang on a hook thing he had to put up in our entrance hall. Anyone who loved me, anyone who even liked me a little bit, would have seen the bees on my stuff and known.

I put my favorite jeans, a couple of tops, my best skirt, my five-year diary which had three years to go, my best glitter pens, my wombat cap Uncle Rob brought me back from Wilson's Promontory, and all my underwear and my frog pajamas in my schoolbag. I took out my old lunch box but left a couple of fruit bars that were right at the bottom.

I wrote a note for Lulu and Fifi:

Dear Lulu and Fifi,
I'm sorry I can't take you with me but I don't know whether I'll end up anywhere guinea pig friendly, so you'll have to stay here for the time being. I hope Dad remembers to feed you. Don't accept anything from the woman. It might be poison. She's the reason I'm running away. She threw away my Bee box and I hate her. I will always hate her because she's hateful and she doesn't even understand who I am and she doesn't care.
Love,
Bee-who-is-never-Beatrice-except-on-the-school-roll.

I didn't run away that night. I don't like the dark much. Running away was scary enough without it being dark.

I ran away early the next morning. It was pretty easy. Jazzi and Dad were still asleep. I put the ten dollars I'd been saving in my pocket, picked up my bag, put the note in Lulu and Fifi's mailbox, made myself a sandwich, and took the rest of the box of fruit bars, a huge piece of carrot cake, and three green apples. I had three pieces of toast for breakfast even though I normally have only two and drank a glass and a half of milk. Then I cleaned my teeth, packed my toothbrush, and simply walked out the door, up the driveway, and onto the road.

It wasn't until I got past the shops—looking into the aquarium shop because I always do—that I realized I couldn't go to Nanna's because she wouldn't be there and I couldn't go to Stan's because he was with Nanna and they were paddling in Lake Jindabyne and eating trout Stan caught from his boat. I couldn't go to Uncle Rob's because I wasn't really sure how to get there. I certainly couldn't go to Lucy's or Sally's because their mothers would send me straight home again.

There was really only one place I could go.

I went back to the shops and used some of my ten dollars on two sticky buns—one with pink icing and one with apple—and then headed for Harley's house.

The lounge chairs had been moved. At first I thought I might have the wrong house, but I knocked at the door anyway and Harley opened it. He had streaks of gray all over his face and there were blobs of paint in his hair.

"To Be!" he said and peered around me. "It's not Wednesday, is it? Have they taken some days away?"

"Jazzi's not here," I said. "And no, it's Saturday. I was wondering if I could use your phone, please. I'm running away."

"There's no phone here," Harley said, "so I'm afraid you can't." I thought he might shut the door on me, so I put my foot firmly against it.

"I brought some sticky buns," I said.

"Do you want to come in?" Harley asked, but he didn't actually open the door any wider.

"Yes, please." I squeezed in under Harley's arm. He smelled a little. Painting is obviously hard work.

"Would you like a cup of tea?"

Harley was obviously ignoring the running away bit. It was a shame about the phone. I wasn't sure how I was going to contact Uncle Rob. I had decided, walking to Harley's, that living with Uncle Rob and Aunty Maree would be the best thing I could do. They were my family, after all. Maybe when Nanna came back I would go and live with her. Then Dad could walk over and see me whenever he wanted to.

"No, thank you. I wouldn't mind a glass of water, though."

Harley looked around wildly. All the glasses I could see had paint water in them, or paintbrushes soaking.

"I could wash one," I offered. I was very thirsty.

"A cup of water, perhaps?"

"That would be fine, thanks. Shall I cut up the buns?"

We sat eating buns. Harley didn't seem to mind which one he ate today. Perhaps that was only a Wednesday thing.

"How's the painting going?" I asked.

"The painting is fine. Arthur is a thorn in my side. No rose, he, but thorns all the way down. He intends to sabotage my work. He has decided he is the chief loony. Why? Because his work is madder than the rest of ours. I should be running away, not you, To Be. Why are you running, anyway?"

"Jazzi threw away my Bee box."

"Your Bee box?"

"You know, a box with things in it that were mine. She didn't really know but she should have. Anyone who called me Bee all the time would know they were Bee things."

"Oh dear." Harley's face crumpled up. "What were the Bee things?"

"Things from when I was little and my mother was alive."

"That's terrible." Harley pushed a big piece of bun onto my plate. "But Jazzi can be like that. She likes to clean and have her own way. She made me run away, too."

"What?"

"Oh, yes. When I was younger, of course, and we lived with our mother. Jazzi didn't believe the things I told her. She said I was making up stories to get out of looking after things. I said she was the looker-afterer but she said I should be, too."

"Hang on, Harley." He was talking so fast I could

hardly catch up. "Why didn't your mum look after things?"

"Some things she looked after, but she worked very hard, so Jasmine was the next looker-afterer. That's how it worked. Jasmine shouted at me because I did things wrongly. So Pepi and I ran away."

"The dog, Pepi?"

"Yes. That was a very wrong wrong thing to do and I was punished—everyone punished me."

"What happened?"

Harley shook his head and stuffed his mouth full of sticky bun.

"Oh, come on, Harley, tell me. As a fellow runner-away."

"It was horrible." Harley spat out bits of icing as he spoke. I pretended not to see, even though it didn't seem to worry Harley.

"Why? What happened?"

"Bad bad bad, dark, rain—too cold, too windy. Couldn't see. The voices were trying to help me but they couldn't get through. Problems in the wires in my head. The rain. It made it too hard to hear them. I tried, in the phone box, but the numbers wouldn't work."

Harley's fingers were drumming on the table, both hands, all of his fingers. He started smacking the table as though it were a bongo drum. He kept chewing his bun, even though I could have sworn he'd swallowed it all.

"Harley," I said as quietly as I could while still being heard above the bongo drum. "Harley, it's okay. That happened years ago, right?"

"It was the beginning," Harley said, "and in the beginning there is always mud and coldness and you never know if you'll be one of the saved or one of the damned. Someone or something dies. I didn't know. I was in the phone box and I didn't know. I was scared, Little Bee, I was too scared to go out of the phone box. I knew I had to stay there until they came to get me— they couldn't hear me because of the rain. So I had to stay there. But I couldn't breathe because there were no windows."

"There aren't windows in phone boxes," I said, "but there aren't doors either."

"There were then. There aren't now but there were then. There were doors and no windows and the door was shut and there was no air coming in and I couldn't make them speak to me through the rain. So I took off my shoe. My good school shoe. The one Jasmine had helped me buy and I tried to make a window myself so I could breathe. They came but the wrong ones came. That was the beginning and it was dark and cold and the dog died."

"What?" This wasn't a story I understood. "Why did the dog die?"

"I can't remember. I can't remember everything.

115

I'm not one of those people who remember. I'm a forgetter most of the time. I forget everything. It's better to forget. They'll let you begin again. Pepi was frightened by the breaking glass, and he ran out onto the road. A car came. See, it's better to forget."

"Oh, Harley, that must have been dreadful."

"It was. It was awful. I shouldn't have taken Pepi. He was Jasmine's dog, not even mine."

I felt a little bit sick. It was the sticky bun, I thought, and too much toast for breakfast.

"Maybe I'll just have to find a phone," I said, getting up. I was going to take my glass and plate to the sink to wash them. That's all I was going to do, but Harley jumped up and grabbed my arms.

"You can't do that," he said fiercely. "I won't let them get you, Little Bee. They'll turn you from To Be to Not to Be. That's what they do. They keep you in rooms like phone boxes and there's no one there except other ones that aren't you but they say you're the same as them and you miss Jasmine who cried and cried but didn't ever stop loving you even after what you'd done. But it wasn't your fault. If there'd been windows you wouldn't have smashed anything. If it hadn't been raining. If it wasn't so dark. You can't go, To Be. You don't want to go there."

He was much bigger than I was and he was holding my arms really tightly. He bent down so his face was too close to mine and I could see the patches where he hadn't shaved very well and little black hairs were bristling out of his skin. But his eyes looked very scared and his mouth sort of looked like mouths do before their owners begin to cry.

"Harley," I said, not moving. "Harley, it's not raining today and it's still very light outside. Is there anyone else here? The people who live here with you, are they here?"

I felt his grip on my arm lessen a little.

"No, they aren't here. They've run away, too. They've run from my drawings. The drawings give us nightmares. But Tony says the drawings are good and need to be drawn. I don't think you need to run away, Little Bee."

"I'll be safe," I told him firmly. "I'm going to Uncle Rob and Aunty Maree's. You've met them. They were at Jazzi's dinner party."

"Jasmine will be so sad. She came to find you and even though you had taken Pepi and Pepi was dead she walked you home, holding your hand. She cried and cried behind her door but she kept looking after you. Your mother got sick because the cancer grew in her. Jasmine will keep crying."

"My mother's dead, Harley, and I haven't taken anything of Jasmine's so she can't be sad. She doesn't even like me."

"No, you're wrong. She will miss you and miss you. She wants someone small like you. Always. And the Worrier, of course, but you, too. She will be scared and sad all over again forever." Harley's chin began to wobble. I knew what that meant. I could almost feel mine start.

"Don't cry, Harley," I said. "Please don't cry."

"You have to take me with you," Harley said. "You have to. The dark and the rain and the sudden lights will come and I won't be able to stop them. Not by myself. Not just me, Harley Raddle. I couldn't before and you're too small, Bee. You're only To Be; you need to be more and bigger."

"Harley," I said, "I think you might be getting sick. Maybe we should both go back together to Jazzi, I mean Jasmine. She'll know what to do, won't she?"

"I can't." Harley dropped my arms and sat right down on the kitchen floor. He drew his knees up under his chin and wrapped his arms around himself as though he were very cold.

"You can," I said, kneeling beside him. "You can, Harley. I know the way and there are no phone boxes at all. We don't need to make a phone call, we can just walk there. You and me together."

"What about the dog?"

"I haven't got a dog, Harley." I thought quickly. I had to make him come with me. I was too worried about him to leave him by himself. "I have these guinea pigs. They're pretty cool. You haven't seen them yet."

Harley was rocking backward and forward, but when I mentioned Fifi and Lulu he stopped for a minute.

"What have guinea pigs got to do with it?"

I shrugged. What had anything got to do with anything? Harley was crying soundlessly now, big tears rolling down his face, streaking the charcoal worse than ever.

"They're pretty good," I said. "They write me notes."

"You're mad," he said. "Guinea pigs don't write notes."

"Mine do," I said.

"You're crazy," he said. "You're not To Be, you've been there, too."

I didn't know what he was talking about, but at least he'd stopped rocking. I stood up and held my hand out to him.

"Come on," I said. "You can meet them."

"I will," he said and took my hand. He was surprisingly heavy to pull up but we managed and I put my bag on my back so he knew I really meant to go. I talked him out of the house. No, Harley, you don't need to bring a tea bag. Yes, Harley, it would be okay to bring a hanky but we need to go now. No, I think your hair looks fine but you might want to wash your face. Okay, if you don't want to, that's fine. It was just an idea. Fifi and Lulu won't mind.

"I have to take the guardian doll," he said just when I thought we were out the front door at last. "If I don't, Jasmine will think I let her die, too."

He darted inside while I tapped my foot on the front step. When he finally emerged again, he was cradling one of Jazzi's dolls in his arms.

"I look after it," he said, "and it should be the other way 'round if it's a guardian doll. I'm always picking it up off the floor." He showed me the face he'd painted on it. It looked sort of like Jazzi, with a mouth that wanted to smile but didn't seem able. He'd painted little hearts, like teardrops, on one cheek. One of her eyes was open and frightened and one was shut with words written across the lid but I didn't have time to read them.

"She's not pretty," he said. "I didn't have to make her pretty."

"She's not pretty," I agreed, "but I don't see why she should be. She's who she is and that's what's important. Let's go."

We had managed to walk half a block, with Harley looking behind him for the darkness and up to the clouds for the rain, so we were walking pretty slowly, when I saw Jazzi's little car zooming toward us. She did a screechy U-turn in front of us.

"Oh, my heavens," she said, getting out all in a rush. "Oh, my goodness. Bee, Harley!" And she ran and hugged us both together, so hard we were all crunched up and I'm sure my elbow went into Harley's stomach but he didn't say anything.

"I think we're safe," Harley told her, pushing her away. "To Be is a Been and she knows what's going on."

"I went to the thrift shop when I got up," Jazzi said, pulling me into her, "and I found the bee skirt. It won't fit you anymore but I wondered if we could make it into a cushion cover. I went home to find you but you weren't there and I was so worried. I went down to Fifi and Lulu and found the note. Then I went back to the shops and that nice woman in the bakery said you'd been in for two sticky buns so I knew where you were and I just flew here as fast as I could. I was so worried."

She was crying and trying to smile at me all at the same time. Her eyes were very wide and frightened, just like the open eye of Harley's doll. For a moment I could see her walking down the dark raining street to find her brother in the smashed phone box. "It's all right," I said. "We're okay, Harley and me."

"I'm not doing another group hug," Harley said. "The last one punched my belly."

"Oh, Harley," Jazzi said and squeezed my shoulders as though I knew what she was sighing for, and she was right, I sort of did.

COCO

*D*ad didn't even know I'd gone and Jazzi asked me not to tell him because she thought he'd think badly of Harley for not coming straight home with me.

"I was so scared," she said. "I thought, if anything has happened to Bee, I'll never ever ever forgive myself. I'm so sorry, Bee, so very sorry, about the box and you seeing Harley like that and everything."

"It's okay," I said, over and over again. "It's really okay, Jazzi."

"He can't help it."

"I know. But we were okay. We were just going to

walk back to you, slowly and calmly. The way you have to with anything scared."

"Oh, Bee, you are so brave and you have so much uncommon sense. I wish, I wish you could like me better. I wish I could be someone you wanted as a . . . you know . . ."

We were sitting at the back of Maxi's Café where no one could see us. Jazzi had rung Dad on her mobile phone and told him we'd be back by lunch, that the shopping was taking a bit longer than she'd expected. She'd sounded all bright and breezy on the phone, but she didn't look like that. She had cried all her makeup off and then she'd had to go to the Ladies' to clean up the smudges. She looked naked and prettier, as if all the crying had washed away more than the makeup.

"I think," I said, putting my hand on hers and noticing for the first time how our fingers were nearly the same length, "that we've misjudged each other. I think maybe we should have told each other more."

"What do you mean?"

"The story about Pepi made me so sad," I told her. "The way he died when the car hit him and Harley was scared to come out of the phone box. That's a real story."

"I don't like to talk about it." Jazzi twisted up the paper napkin so it was a spiral. "I like things to be perfect."

I remembered her dinner party and the glasses glowing in the candlelight. "You can make some things look beautiful," I said, "but other things are just different. Like Harley's doll. You made that and the dress is perfect but he had to paint on the face he wanted. Just like my Bee box had stuff in it that didn't look good to anyone else."

"I'm sorry about your Bee box. If I'd known. Or if I'd paid more attention. It's all my fault. I want so much for Nick and me and you to be happy together."

I knew that one day I'd tell Dad what happened, because it was a true story and you have to tell those when you can. But for the time being I was content to do it Jazzi's way. When we got home we didn't talk about me running away or calling Tony, Harley's doctor, and getting Harley to take his pills. We didn't talk about Pepi, who ran onto the road and got killed. I didn't tell Dad that Jazzi had written the guinea pig letters to me, but I read them all again because they were like seeing Jazzi without her makeup on and I liked that.

"You know how it's Jazzi's birthday soon," I said to Dad that night when he tucked me into bed.

"Is it? Oh, Bee, what would I do without you to remind me about these things!"

"Well, I've thought of a present," I said. "I know she'd really love it."

"Yes?"

"A dog. A little kind of dog. Not too little and not yappy but not a big dog either. Something medium-sized with soft fur."

"Are you sure this isn't a Bee present dressed up to look like a Jazzi present?"

"Honest, Dad. I love puppies, of course, but this would have to be Jazzi's dog. I'll help look after it but it would belong to her."

"Well, I suppose all kids should have a dog in their lives at some stage and you are old enough."

I rolled my eyes but I didn't say anything because in the end it didn't matter. Jazzi and I and the dog would know who really owned it and if we all loved it, well, isn't that better anyway?

I chose the dog, of course, because I knew exactly what I was looking for. She was little but not too little. She wasn't a complete breed of anything but she looked as though she could have been. She had the kind of fur you wanted to stroke. It was soft, not hard, and it was kind of gray and kind of brown. She had long eyelashes and floppy ears and a little curled tail that she wagged all the time.

Jazzi named the dog Coco, after Coco Chanel who designed dresses years ago and also to fit in with Fifi and Lulu who were guinea pigs with a French accent.

I woke up on the morning after Jazzi's birthday to find, written on my mirror in Jazzi's plum lipstick: *Coco, Fifi, and Lulu, ze three musketeers, rule ze world!* I didn't clean it off for ages, because it made me smile every time I read it.